WATER WINGS

Born in the UK, Morris Gleitzman emigrated to Australia with his family at the age of sixteen. His career took off as a screenwriter and a newspaper columnist, before he became a successful author. He has written a number of children's books, including *Two Weeks with the Queen*, *Belly Flop*, *Blabber Mouth* and *Sticky Beak*. He lives in Melbourne and has two children.

Visit Morris Gleitzman's website
at www.morrisgleitzman.com

Praise for *Water Wings*:

'Will make you laugh and cry.'
Young Telegraph

'Morris Gleitzman is in dazzling form.'
Lindsey Fraser, *Scotsman*

'This is one not to be missed.'
Tony Bradman, *Daily Telegraph*

'Gleitzman is amusing and down to earth . . . magnificent.'
Michele Hanson, *Mail on Sunday*

'An extraordinaryly clever mix of humour and sorrow. You will cry, certainly, but you will also laugh out loud as the characters never ask for sympathy, but share with the reader their huge enjoyment of life. A truly special book.'
Valerie Birman, *Carousel*

Morris Gleitzman

Water Wings

First published 1996 by Pan Macmillan Publishers Australia
First published in the UK 1997 by Pan Macmillan Children's Books

This edition published 2001 by Macmillan Children's Books
a division of Macmillan Publishers Limited
20 New Wharf Road, London N1 9RR
Basingstoke and Oxford
www.panmacmillan.com

Associated companies throughout the world

ISBN 0 330 39825 3

3 5 7 9 8 6 4 2

A CIP catalogue record for this book is available from
the British Library.

Printed and bound in Great Britain by Mackays of Chatham plc, Kent

Chapter One

'What I need,' said Pearl, as she started to slide off the roof, 'is a grandmother.'

There weren't any around, so Pearl grabbed hold of the TV aerial instead.

Then a thought hit her.

She looked anxiously down at the driveway.

If she fell, she didn't want to fall on Winston.

He was the kindest bravest guinea pig in the whole world, but if he tried to catch her he'd also be the flattest.

Pearl could see him directly below, a fluffy black-and-white blob, peering up at her, nose twitching with concern.

'Winston,' she called, 'shift over there next to the herb tub.'

Winston didn't move.

He gave her a few encouraging squeaks.

Pearl braced her feet against the tin roof, gripped the aerial as hard as she could and leant out over the guttering so Winston could see her pointing at the clump of basil.

A gust of wind nearly blew her off.

'Winston,' she yelled, 'it's not safe. Move.'

Winston moved.

He hurled himself at the wall and tried to run up the drainpipe, feet scrabbling on the shiny paint.

Then he slowly slid back down.

Pearl couldn't help grinning, even though her heart was scrabbling inside her chest.

'Winston,' she croaked, 'forget what I said. Stay where you are, OK?'

Winston stayed.

Only his ears moved, trembling in the wind.

Pearl grinned even wider and felt her guts unclench.

What a dope.

He'd tried to rescue her.

Even though he didn't have ropes or pulleys or a fire truck with an extension ladder, he'd still tried to rescue her.

She wanted to climb down and hug him.

But first she had a job to do.

Mum's bra.

Pearl squinted across the roof.

There it was, flapping white against the chimney.

'Alright you dumb bra,' said Pearl, 'here I come.'

Legs trembling, she pushed herself up the sloping tin.

She could hear her shirt buttons scraping on the metal, and the rubber on her shoes squeaking like Winston when he got indignant.

'If you had a grandma,' Winston would be squeaking if he was up here now, 'you wouldn't have to risk your neck like this.'

Too right, thought Pearl, edging towards the dancing bra. If I had a grandma she'd teach me all sorts of stuff.

How to knit a jumper for a guinea pig.

How to write to Dad when I don't know where he lives.

How to peg Mum's bras on the line so they don't get blown onto the roof.

That's what Grandmas are for.

To teach you all the stuff busy Mums don't have time to.

Plus make you birthday cakes and help you get the guinea pig poo out of your hair and cuddle you once in a while and . . .

Pearl blinked hard.

This was no time to get distracted.

She wrapped an arm round the chimney and leant over as far as she could and grabbed the bra with her fingertips.

Just as well it's a 38D, thought Pearl.

She pitied kids with skinny mums. Grabbing small bras off windy roofs must be really hard.

She gripped the bra between her teeth and started to climb down.

A sports car that sounded like Mum's screeched round the corner at the end of the street.

Pearl squinted down.

Yes, it was Mum. There were only three red Capris in the whole town and Mum was the only one whose numberplate said CAR4ME.

Suddenly Pearl's heart started going scrabbly again.

There was a bloke sitting next to Mum.

It must be Howard.

'Winston,' Pearl called down excitedly. 'She's brought him home.'

Winston frowned at the approaching car.

'Don't be cross with her,' said Pearl. 'She had to wait a few weeks for the relationship to develop. New blokes can be put off if they find out there's a kid and a guinea pig.'

Winston's face softened.

As the car pulled up, Pearl peered at Howard. He didn't look like he'd be put off too easily.

Pearl shivered with excitement and felt for the drainpipe with her feet.

'So, Pearl,' said Howard. 'This must be Winston.'

'That's right,' said Pearl.

Winston waddled across the carpet, sniffed Howard's squash shoe and gave it a friendly chew.

'Hello Winston,' said Howard, taking a step back. 'Haven't you got a cage then?'

Pearl left Winston to explain that he was a free-range guinea pig who liked to roam proud and unrestrained, plus when he did flake out it was in a hutch.

While Winston squeaked earnestly, Pearl checked Howard for grey hairs.

None on his head.

None on his legs either, what she could see of them between his squash socks and his shorts.

Excellent, thought Pearl. He can't be more than thirty-five.

Winston gave an impatient squeak.

OK Winston, calm down, she thought. I'm going to ask him the question now.

She took a deep breath.

Before she could speak, Mum came out of the bathroom in a towel.

'Pearl, don't pester Howard,' she said, rummaging in the washing basket. 'Let him have a shower. We're due at the restaurant in half an hour.'

Howard kissed Mum on the cheek and went into the bathroom.

Mum put her face close to Pearl's.

'He's the best thing that's happened to me since your Dad left,' she said. 'Don't blow it for me, OK?'

Pearl stared at her, puzzled.

Mum held a bra up in front of Pearl's face. It had sooty streaks on it, and a bit of dribble.

'Can't trust you with anything, can I?' said Mum.

Pearl sighed.

Nibble. Nibble. Nibble.

Pearl opened her eyes.

It was still dark.

Strange, she thought.

Winston hardly ever nibbled her ear in the dark. He usually waited till the sun was up and peeping through the dump trucks on her curtains.

Pearl sat up, straining to hear if the house was burning down.

It wasn't.

Then she heard Mum and Howard at the front door, giggling while Mum tried to get the key in the lock.

Pearl gave Winston a grateful kiss on the tummy.

'Thanks,' she whispered. 'I was out like a light. Dunno what I'd do without you Winston.'

Winston squeaked softly in her ear. Something about getting on with asking Howard the question and not wasting time being drippy.

'Good point,' Pearl whispered, and listened carefully as Mum and Howard banged the front door shut behind them.

After a bit she heard Mum go into her room and Howard clump into the bathroom.

Pearl slipped out of bed and crept along the hallway.

The bathroom door was open.

She peeped in.

Howard was at the sink, shirt unbuttoned, splashing Mum's eau de cologne under his arms.

'Howard,' said Pearl softly.

Howard jumped and dropped the bottle.

It smashed.

He spun round.

'Jeez!' he shouted. 'Don't creep up on a bloke like that.'

Pearl opened her mouth to apologise but it was too late. Mum was storming towards her, dress half undone.

'What are you doing out of bed?' she demanded.

Pearl started to tell her, then decided not to.

Mum wasn't even listening anyway, she was doing her speech about how parents who run busy offices for twelve hours a day deserve a couple of hours off at night without kids making them break the zips on their dresses.

Howard crouched down next to Pearl.

'Did you have a nightmare?' he asked.

'She doesn't have nightmares,' said Mum. 'I'm the one who has nightmares. That cologne cost sixty-eight dollars.'

Pearl sighed.

As soon as the toast popped up, Pearl put it on the plates and checked the rest of the tray.

Tomato juice, Coco Pops, scrambled eggs, strawberry milk and toast.

It was her first breakfast tray and she wanted it to be a good one.

'Shame there's no bacon,' she said. 'Still, this is almost as good, eh?'

Winston sniffed the fish fingers and looked doubtful.

'OK,' said Pearl, 'I know you think they'd prefer frozen peas and sweetcorn, but not everyone likes that as much as you.'

Pearl picked up the tray and carried it carefully to Mum's room.

She peered in.

Good.

Mum and Howard were still asleep.

'Remember,' she whispered to Winston, 'if

Mum wakes up we're just bringing her a break-fast tray, OK?'

Winston squeaked OK.

Good on you Winston, thought Pearl. Winston'd never dob on her, not even if he was being tortured with bulldog clips on his whiskers.

She pushed the door open with her bottom and carried the tray over to where Howard lay on his tummy, face half buried in the pillow.

She knelt down and put her face close to his ear.

'Howard,' she whispered, 'I need to ask you something.'

'Mmmmmpflbbb,' moaned Howard.

'Your mum ... is she still alive?'

'Ggggnslfff,' groaned Howard.

'The reason I'm asking,' continued Pearl, 'is cause my mum and dad's parents died before I was born, so I haven't got an actual real grandma of my own but if your mum's still alive she'd technically be my grandma, as long as you and Mum are serious about each other.'

Pearl noticed the smudges of lipstick on Howard's face.

It looked like he and Mum were serious about each other all right.

'So,' whispered Pearl urgently, 'is she dead yet?'

'Zzzzgnkkk,' gurgled Howard, and his arm slipped off the edge of the bed and fell into the scrambled eggs.

His eyes snapped open.

'Ow!' he yelled.

He pulled his burnt hand off the plate, knocking a glass of tomato juice over Winston.

Pearl watched horrified as Winston gave a loud squeak, leaped off the tray and burrowed under the bedclothes.

'Arghhh!' screamed Mum, sitting up wildly. 'It's a snake!'

Winston peered out indignantly from the bottom of the sheet.

Pearl grabbed him and held him close to her.

There was a long silence while Mum and Howard stared bleary-eyed around the room.

Finally they focused on Pearl.

'Breakfast in bed,' Pearl said weakly, pointing to the tray. 'Hope you like fish fingers.'

There was another long silence while Mum and Howard stared at the tray.

'Jeez,' said Howard at last. 'Pretty noisy room service. I reckon most of Australia's awake now. Including my mother and she's sixty-eight and going deaf.'

Pearl and Winston looked at each other delightedly.

Pearl had a wonderful vision of the delicious

breakfast trays they'd soon be sharing in bed with their new grandma.

Homemade cakes, probably.

Maybe even homemade Coco Pops.

And cow weed scones for Winston.

A noise interrupted Pearl's thoughts.

It was Mum sighing crossly.

'Next time you get a bright idea like this,' said Mum, 'check with me first. And you know I don't allow that animal in here.'

Winston waddled out of the room.

Pearl followed, trying very hard not to do cartwheels.

Chapter Two

'Two thousand kilometres?'

Pearl stared at Mum in horror.

'She lives way out in Woop Woop,' said Mum absently, sipping her coffee and running her eyes over some business papers. 'Howard hasn't seen her for yonks. Eat your breakfast or you'll be late for thingy.'

'School,' said Pearl sadly.

She put another spoonful of Coco Pops into her mouth.

Disappointment made them taste like the dried sow-thistle she fed Winston for his bowels.

It wasn't fair.

All her life she'd waited for a grandma and now she'd finally got one, the dopey old chook lived too far away.

Pearl saw Winston frowning at her.

'I know, I know,' she sighed. 'It's not her fault

where she lives. Just makes it a bit hard to invite her to school open days, that's all.'

Mum grunted to herself and scribbled something onto a page of figures.

Winston gave Pearl a sympathetic look.

Except, she noticed, it wasn't the same as his usual sympathetic look.

His cheeks were more scrunched, almost as if he was in pain.

And he'd done a pee in the butter dish, which he'd never done before.

'You OK?' asked Pearl.

She saw he hadn't touched his breakfast, not the rolled oats or the dried fruit or the lucerne fibre or the strawberry milk.

Winston gave her an 'I'm fine' squeak, but Pearl knew he was just being brave.

A person was bound to be feeling a bit under the weather when they'd just been half-drowned in tomato juice.

From the shower came the distant sound of Howard singing.

Winston gave a little shudder.

And that's not helping, thought Pearl.

Winston had never liked opera.

Winston gave a grunt and waggled his bottom in the direction of the bathroom.

For a sec Pearl thought he was just being a critic, then she realised he was trying to tell her an idea.

A really good idea.

'Good on you Winston,' said Pearl. 'Spot on.'

Mum looked up irritably from her sales sheets.

'Did you say something?' she asked.

'I'm going to see if Howard wants to go to my school open day,' said Pearl.

Mum sighed wearily.

'Howard hasn't got time for open days,' she said. 'He's got a business to run. He's a vet. The only one in town, so he's very busy.'

Pearl stared at her.

How could a bloke be a vet when he didn't even know the difference between a cage and a hutch?

Pearl listened to Howard trying to hit a high note in the shower and felt glad Winston had never needed a vet.

No way would she leave him at the mercy of a bloke who'd spent all his training years at the opera.

'Anyway,' said Mum, 'you don't need Howard to go to the school open day because I'm going. When is it?'

'This morning,' said Pearl quietly. 'Ten o'clock.'

Mum sighed again and typed something into her electronic personal organiser.

Pearl took a deep breath.

'Mum,' she said, 'I know you're really busy so if you're not going to be able to make it, that's OK, but I'd rather know now.'

Mum frowned at her crossly.

'Pearl,' she said, 'watch my lips. I'll be there.'

'And this,' said Pearl proudly, pointing up at the wall, 'is my project on guinea pigs.'

She looked anxiously at the pages to make sure Mr Gallico had stuck them up in the right order.

Then she held her breath, waiting for a response.

Winston stared at the project and didn't say anything.

Perhaps he can't see it properly, thought Pearl.

She lifted Winston up a bit so his whole head was sticking out of her school bag.

Winston flattened his ears, which Pearl knew meant he was concentrating, and blinked at the pages.

Then he gave several low whistles.

Pearl breathed a sigh of relief.

It was always nerve-racking, having your work assessed by an expert.

Particularly when other kids and parents and grandparents were pointing and giggling.

'Pearl,' said a loud voice, 'I don't think I've met your guest.'

Pearl tried to slide Winston back inside her bag.

Too late.

Mr Gallico had snuck up on her behind the egg-carton tribal masks.

'Thank you Pearl,' he said, gesturing for her to hand Winston over.

Pearl froze, heart going frantic.

Last week when Mr Gallico had confiscated Ewan Foley's dart gun, he'd chucked it in the bin.

'Thank you, Pearl,' said Mr Gallico more loudly.

He reached down for Winston.

Before she let go, Pearl gave Winston a reassuring squeeze just to let him know that he wouldn't be spending more than two seconds in the bin, even if it got her expelled.

Winston gave a loud whistle.

It was almost a scream.

Pearl had never heard him do that before.

'Be gentle with him,' she begged. 'He's scared.'

She hoped desperately that Mr Gallico had a secret soft spot for guinea pigs. He might. He looked a bit like one himself.

Mr Gallico held Winston in a pudgy hand and they studied each other.

Then Mr Gallico looked sternly at Pearl.

'Is your mother here?' he asked.

'No,' said Pearl quietly. 'She must have got busy. She's a general manager.'

A woman standing nearby shook her head.

'We're all busy,' she muttered to her friend, 'but some of us put our kids first.'

Pearl saw that many of the parents and grandparents were nodding and looking at her pityingly.

'This is the busiest time of year for a tobacco co-op,' Pearl explained to them. 'All the farmers are sending their tobacco in for Mum to sell. If she neglects her job, this town could go broke.'

The parents and grandparents thought about this.

'The fact remains,' said Mr Gallico, 'open day is for family members and relatives, not pets.'

'Winston is a family member,' said Pearl. 'He's been in my family for years.'

'He's still an animal,' said Mr Gallico.

Pearl wished she could cover Winston's ears.

'He's a mammal,' she said. 'He's the same as everyone else here.'

She looked around at the parents and grandparents, hoping they'd agree.

They didn't.

Nor did Mr Gallico.

'There are many differences between animals and humans,' he said, voice rising with anger, 'one of them being where they go to the toilet.'

A titter ran round the classroom.

Pearl stared in horror at the liquid trickling through Mr Gallico's fingers.

She couldn't believe it.

Winston had never done that before.

Mr Gallico picked Winston up with his dry hand and thrust him at Pearl.

Before she could take him, Mr Gallico spotted a large wet patch on his trousers and let go too early.

Winston dropped to the floor.

The classroom echoed with the loudest squeal Pearl had ever heard.

For a sec she thought it was Mum slamming on her brakes in the playground.

But it wasn't, it was Winston.

Pearl grabbed the key from the herb tub, barged the front door open and sprinted into her room.

'Nearly there,' she panted to the school bag cradled in her arms.

Winston looked up at her gratefully.

Pearl stuffed fresh hay into the sleeping compartment of his hutch and laid him gently onto it.

'You're home now,' she said.

She watched him burrow in.

Her hands shook with relief.

It had been the worst afternoon of her life, even though Mr Gallico had apologised and said not to worry about the dry cleaning and had let Winston spend the rest of the day in a book box full of egg carton offcuts where he'd gone to sleep.

Which was pretty unusual for Winston.

Pearl had felt sick.

She'd just wanted the bell to ring so she could get him home.

Now she put her face close to the hutch.

'If you end up with a limp from this,' she said softly, 'we'll sue him.'

Winston squeaked his agreement.

Pearl peered at him even more closely.

Had his squeak sounded strange or was she just overanxious?

The phone rang.

Pearl ignored it.

Mum's voice boomed out through the answering machine.

'Sorry Pearl,' she said. 'Absolute chaos this end. I tried to get away this morning but some ciggie bigwigs turned up unexpectedly and I had to take them to lunch. I'm glad I did because . . .'

Pearl stopped listening.

All she could do was stare in horror.

In the hutch Winston had fallen onto his side, his legs stiff, his whole body trembling.

'Do you have an appointment?' asked the nurse.

Pearl, gasping for breath, held the plastic bowl with Winston in it under the nurse's nose.

She knew the nurse would understand when she saw Winston peeping out of the straw, sad and quivering and in pain.

The nurse gently pushed the bowl away.

'The vet has several people waiting,' she said. 'He'll see you as soon as he can.'

Pearl put the bowl onto the counter so she wouldn't jolt Winston when she blew her top.

'Please tell the vet it's an emergency,' she said, 'and if he doesn't come now, Mum won't ever let him use her deodorant again.'

The waiting room fell silent.

Three people, two budgerigars and a German shepherd stared at Pearl.

The nurse obviously didn't know Mum.

Instead of saying 'she'd be too busy to notice', the nurse picked up the phone and spoke to Howard.

The next ten minutes felt like ten hours.

First Howard finished examining a ginger cat.

Then he told Pearl to stay in the waiting room while he took Winston into his surgery.

Pearl stood outside the surgery door, straining to hear what was going on inside.

She'd just started to apologise to the people and the budgies and the German shepherd when she heard Winston squeal.

She flung herself into the surgery.

Winston was lying on a table, trembling.

Howard was holding a glass tube against his white sleeve and studying the liquid in it.

He looked up, startled.

'Jeez,' he said crossly. 'Do you want me to drop this one as well?'

'Is Winston OK?' asked Pearl.

Her throat felt so desperate she could hardly force the words out.

Winston gave her a pleading look.

Pearl hoped it was just because Howard had been singing.

Howard put the glass tube down.

'How old is Winston?' he asked.

'Six,' said Pearl. 'Seven on August the nineteenth. Dad gave him to me for my birthday, just before he left.'

Howard sat down at his desk and started writing on a pad.

'As guinea pigs become temporally advanced,' he said, 'they can develop a bilateral renal nephrosis. There can be tubular atrophy, interstitial fibrosis and sometimes acute neoplasia.'

Pearl stared at him.

This was worse than Japanese at school.

Howard looked up at her and his face softened.

'I'll send Winston's wee off for tests to make sure,' he said, 'but I think you're going to have to be a very brave girl. It looks like his kidneys are pretty serious.'

Pearl's head was ringing with panic.

'You mean,' she heard herself croak, 'he's got to have a kidney transplant?'

Howard shook his head.

Pearl felt relief flood through her.

Winston looked pretty relieved too.

'Guinea pigs can't have kidney transplants,' said Howard. 'When renal disease is this advanced, it's time to say goodbye.'

Pearl gaped at him.

He was speaking Japanese again.

'Winston won't suffer,' said Howard softly. 'Two little needles and he won't feel any more pain.'

Pearl stood frozen for a long time.

Then she gently picked Winston up, kissed him, and ran out of the surgery with him as fast as she could.

Chapter Three

'Leeks?' said Craigette Benson, twisting her bedroom curtains in her hands. 'We haven't got any leeks.'

'OK, green capsicums,' said Pearl desperately, chopping broccoli as fast as she could. 'Green capsicums are good for the kidneys.'

Craigette didn't move.

'Come on,' pleaded Pearl. 'Your Dad's got a fruit shop. Look in the fridge.'

'You've had everything from the fridge,' said Craigette miserably. 'There's nothing green left in the fridge except lime cordial.'

Pearl took a deep breath.

Stay calm, she told herself, for Winston's sake.

She stroked Winston's cheek.

'Don't worry,' she whispered to him, carefully placing some crumbs of broccoli next to his mouth. 'If you can't eat this, we'll get you some leeks.'

Winston didn't say anything.

He just lay on Craigette's bed shivering under the duvet.

'Don't promise him leeks,' said Craigette, 'cause there aren't any.'

Pearl saw that the shivering was getting worse.

She turned away so Winston wouldn't see her face if she panicked.

'Craigette, please,' she said. 'Winston urgently needs vitamins for his kidneys. We've got to find something he can eat.'

Craigette wasn't even paying attention. She was peering anxiously out of the window.

'My parents'll kill us if they find you here,' she said. 'I'm not even allowed to eat lollies in my room, let alone prepare vegies.'

Pearl felt a strong urge to hit Craigette with the chopping board.

Then she saw that Winston was ignoring the broccoli, just like he had the lettuce, french beans, bok choy, beetroot tops, celery, sweet corn and frozen peas.

'Come on,' she begged Winston. 'Eat something.'

'There's beetroot on my wallpaper,' said Craigette miserably. 'My parents'll kill us.'

She dabbed at the wall with a tissue.

Pearl put a crumb of broccoli on her finger and held it to Winston's lips.

'Just try one bit,' she said. 'If you're too weak to chew, just suck it.'

She held her breath, praying he would.

'Oh no,' moaned Craigette, 'celery in my slippers.'

Winston looked up at Pearl with moist eyes.

'And lettuce under my pillow,' said Craigette. 'Yuk.'

Pearl took a desperate breath.

What if Howard was right?

What if Winston wasn't going to get better?

In the distance the doorbell rang.

Craigette hurried out of the room.

That's all we need, thought Pearl. Angry parents who don't understand how dangerous yelling can be for a sick guinea pig.

She put her mouth close to Winston's ear.

'We've got to shift,' she said urgently. 'I'm taking you to . . .'

She thought frantically.

'. . . to a shack in the bush. With an old stove so I can make you grass and thistle soup.'

While she tried to remember if she'd ever come across any shacks with working stoves within walking distance of town, Pearl began to gently lift Winston out from under the duvet.

He squealed with pain.

Heart scrabbling, Pearl slid him back under the cover and stroked his quivering fur.

He looked up at her anxiously.

'It's OK,' she said, her own throat aching with worry. 'Don't worry about Craigette's parents. Fruit shop owners have to help people with vitamin deficiencies, it's the law.'

She heard footsteps behind her and turned.

But it wasn't Mr and Mrs Benson.

It was Mum and Howard.

'It's a tragedy,' said Mum, overtaking an ambulance, 'and we feel for you, love. But we do not have time for these hide-and-seek games.'

'And it's not fair on Winston,' said Howard. 'He was in a lot of pain. You should be grateful your friend rang us.'

In the back seat Pearl didn't say anything.

She imagined a giant slug crawling out of a lettuce in the fruit shop and eating Craigette.

It didn't make her feel any better, so she went back to concentrating on how Winston was feeling.

He lay on her lap, his head cradled in her hands.

Not moving.

'That injection,' said Pearl, 'was just to make him feel better, right?'

'Yes,' said Howard patiently, 'it was just to control the pain.'

Pearl didn't take her eyes off Winston.

You'd better be telling the truth, she thought.

She wondered how many horse tranquillisers it would take to kill a vet.

'Pearl,' said Mum, 'I've been thinking. How would you like a mobile phone?'

'If Howard wants to kill Winston,' said Pearl, 'he'll have to kill me first.'

'OK,' said Mum, 'it was just a suggestion.'

Pearl knew it was hopeless as soon as she saw the long words on the lab report.

Hands shaking, she went over to the surgery table and showed the print-out to Winston.

He looked at it and then looked up at her.

She could tell he understood.

Howard put his arm round Pearl's shoulder.

'Think of it this way,' he said softly. 'With a wonderful owner like you he's hardly suffered in his whole life. Shame to make him start now, just for the sake of a couple of weeks.'

Pearl tried to ask Howard if there was any way of transplanting something from her body to Winston's, but she couldn't speak.

'Because that's all it'd be,' he said. 'A couple of weeks of pointless pain and misery.'

The sadness in her throat was almost choking her.

'Or I can put him gently to sleep,' said Howard, 'and he won't feel a thing. Which do you think he'd prefer?'

Winston gave a tiny squeak.

Pearl looked into his pleading eyes and saw his answer.

But she had to be sure.

She pressed her lips against the fur on his cheek and strained to hear if he was squeaking anything about wanting heaps more vitamins or a shack in the bush.

He wasn't.

Pearl said goodbye quickly.

She was worried the first injection would wear off and she didn't want to risk Winston being in agony again.

Plus she didn't want to upset him with loads of crying.

It was bad enough for him knowing the second needle was waiting on the work surface.

So she just hugged him gently for a while and thanked him for being the best friend she'd ever had.

She could tell from his expression he felt the same about her.

Then Howard and the nurse came in.

'All ready?' said Howard.

Somehow Pearl made herself nod.

'Come on Pearl,' said the nurse, 'I'll make you a cup of tea.'

Pearl sat down and held Winston to her chest.

He blinked up at her gratefully.

She looked into his eyes.

'I'm sorry,' she whispered.

She saw that Winston understood.

'Do it now,' she said.

Afterwards, Mum arrived.

'You poor love,' she said, and put her arms round Pearl.

'She was very brave,' said the nurse.

'Not a tear,' said Howard.

'Takes after me,' said Mum.

Pearl didn't bother trying to tell Mum that she'd been crying for twenty minutes in the toilet.

She was too numb to speak.

'We'll have a funeral,' said Mum. 'Just as soon as I've dropped some clients off at the airport. Just you and me.'

'Where?' whispered Pearl, but Mum was already on her way to the carpark.

Pearl showed Winston the hole she'd dug.

'Sorry it's not much of a grave,' she said,

tilting him so his head pointed towards it.

She knew Winston couldn't actually see it, but showing him made her feel better.

Just a bit.

She was glad Winston couldn't see it because he'd probably feel offended at being buried in a herb tub.

'It was the only place I could dig,' she said. 'When Mum had the backyard brick paved to make it low maintenance, she didn't think to leave space for a grave.'

Pearl looked down the street for the hundredth time.

Still no Mum.

'Sorry it's not much of a funeral either,' she said. 'Mum must have been held up.'

She hugged Winston to her.

Even though he was going cold and stiff, his fur still smelt like Winston.

'At least I've got you for company,' she said.

But not for much longer.

Not once he was in the herb tub.

She stared at the dark damp hole for a long time.

Then she dried her tears.

'There's no way I'm putting you in there Winston,' she said.

She filled the hole in loosely so there was a mound and stuck in the cross she'd made from two of the roof supports from Winston's hutch.

Then she carried Winston into the kitchen, opened the freezer, and laid him carefully at the back under the peas and sweet corn he loved so much.

Chapter Four

'It's a crisis,' said Mum, plonking an armful of business papers and takeaway on the kitchen table. 'Barely two weeks till the Tobacco Carnival and the Carnival Queen writes her car off.'

Pearl tried to look sympathetic.

'Extensive whiplash,' said Mum. 'Doctor says she'll be in bed for a month. I asked him if there was any way we could prop her up on the float, but he said no chance.'

Mum sighed and stared at the paperwork, lost in thought.

Then she remembered something.

'Oh no,' she said, 'have I missed the funeral?'

Pearl nodded.

'Sorry,' said Mum.

She started unwrapping the takeaway.

'Let's eat,' she said, 'and then you can show

me where you've buried him. Do you want peas or corn with your burger?'

'I don't really feel like vegies,' said Pearl quietly, leaning against the freezer door.

'I was hoping you'd say that,' said Mum.

Mum stared at the herb tub, mouth open.

'There wasn't anywhere else to dig,' said Pearl.

'But . . . what about my herbs?' screeched Mum.

'I put them all back in,' said Pearl. 'They'll be fine. Things always grow extra well in grave-yards.'

Mum looked ill.

For a fleeting second Pearl was tempted to put Mum out of her misery and tell her to look in the freezer.

She didn't.

It'd be suicide.

Winston would probably end up in the garbage or somewhere.

'You could have buried him at school,' said Mum, exasperated. 'Or at Howard's place. He's got a big garden.'

Pearl blinked hard to keep the tears in.

Mum might have an important job, but she didn't know much about death.

Or daughters.

Pearl had just turned her light out and was about

to have a cry when Mum came in and sat on the bed.

She took Pearl's hand.

I don't believe it, thought Pearl. It's been years since she did anything like this.

Despite everything, Pearl felt a warm feeling creep into her chest.

It didn't stay long.

'What I've decided to do,' said Mum, 'is go to Sydney and sign up a Carnival Queen there. A soapie actor or something like that. I'm not risking another town girl.'

Pearl stared at Mum in the darkness.

'It'll only be for a few days,' said Mum. 'Howard's getting a locum in to mind the surgery and he's coming with me cause he's got a mate who works in telly. So we'll need to find someone for you to stay with. One of the girls at school.'

Pearl didn't say anything.

She bit her lip to stop herself.

It wouldn't be fair saying what she wanted to say to a mother with such a heavy workload.

But the words came out anyway.

'Mum,' said Pearl quietly. 'Don't go. I'm really sad and I need you.'

Mum gave an exasperated sigh.

'Love,' she said, 'I have to. You know how important the Tobacco Carnival is to this town. And to my job. Don't do this to me.'

'Sorry,' said Pearl.

Mum squeezed Pearl's hand so hard it hurt.

'You choose someone to stay with,' said Mum, 'OK?'

Pearl lay in the darkness for a long time and let thoughts run through her mind and tears run down her cheeks.

Then she switched on her light and looked for a pen and some paper.

Dear Grandma, she wrote.

Hope you don't mind me calling you that, but as your son and my mum are going out together, I think it's the legal word.

Can I come and live with you?

I know this is a bit sudden, but there's nothing left for me here.

My best friend in the whole world died today which just leaves Mum and she's very busy and doesn't really have time for me. It's not her fault, it happens sometimes when you're a chief executive and sole breadwinner.

I haven't got any other grandmas or grandpas and Dad lives overseas somewhere but he won't tell us where.

I'm very good at breakfast trays, and am willing to learn embroidery and walking frame maintenance and anything else you might need a hand with.

Please reply soon and I'll come straight away.

Your new grand daughter,

Pearl Woziak

PS I can only come if you've got a freezer.

Pearl crept out to the kitchen to show Winston. The ice on his fur made him look old and grey and wise, and even though she knew he couldn't actually read what she'd written, she was sure he would have approved.

'Howard,' said Pearl, 'do you have your mother's full name and address? I want to invite her to my school open day next year.'

Mum snorted into her Chinese takeaway.

Howard grinned through a mouthful of fried rice.

'I can probably remember it,' he said. 'Don't hold your breath for a reply, though. Sometimes she takes months.'

'Oh,' said Pearl. 'OK, have you got her number? I'll give her a ring.'

'You probably won't get through at the moment,' said Howard. 'They were flooded out up there last week and the phone lines are still affected. You could fax my brother-in-law. He's with the bank up there and they can use the army line.'

Pearl thought about soldiers and loans officers reading her letter to Grandma.

'Thanks,' she said, 'but I'll post it.'

Mum snapped her fingers.

'Here's an idea,' she said to Howard. 'Your

mother could come and babysit Pearl while we're away.'

Pearl thought about this.

It'd be a good way to get to know Grandma before actually moving in with her.

Then she realised Howard was choking on a prawn.

'No chance,' he spluttered. 'Wouldn't get her down here with a bulldozer. She hates this town. Reckons she won't ever set foot here again.'

Pity, thought Pearl. Still, probably for the best. I'm looking for a permanent relationship and a new life, not a babysitter.

'Pity,' said Mum. 'We're not exactly being flooded with offers of accommodation from Pearl's friends.'

'OK Winston,' whispered Pearl, 'this is it.'

She looked up to make sure nobody was coming out of the post office, then lifted Winston out of her schoolbag and touched his nose onto the letter for good luck.

'Thanks Winston,' she said.

Winston had always liked to touch things with his warm nose for luck, and Pearl didn't see why this should change just because his nose was minus four degrees centigrade.

She took a step towards the post box.

'G'day Pearl, whatcha got there?'

Pearl's guts dropped to minus four degrees centigrade.

It was Craigette and some of the girls from school.

Pearl tried to slip Winston back into her schoolbag.

Too late.

They'd seen him.

'Jeez,' said Craigette, coming over, 'look at the size of that ice lolly.'

The girls crowded round.

'That's not an ice lolly.'

'It's hairy.'

'Give us a look.'

Then Craigette recognised Winston and screamed.

The rest of the girls stopped dead, eyes wide with horror.

Pearl was glad Winston couldn't see them.

'It's a perfectly normal scientific process,' she said indignantly. 'Heaps of people are frozen until medical science works out how to cure them in the future. You can pat him if you like.'

The girls backed away.

'You're sick,' said Craigette.

'Yuk,' said one of the other girls to Craigette, 'and you let her into your house.'

'Never again,' said Craigette.

Pearl watched them hurry away down the street making loud retching noises and giving her disgusted looks.

Then she touched Winston's nose on the letter again for double luck.

'We're going to need it,' said Pearl. 'Grandma's our last hope.'

Chapter Five

'It's been a week and still no reply,' said Pearl miserably. 'I guess she doesn't want me.'

She stroked the frost off Winston's eyebrows.

She knew he'd give her a sympathetic look if he could.

And a cheery squeak.

Pearl tried to cheer herself up.

Perhaps Grandma never got the letter, she thought. Perhaps her postman was swept away by a mud slide.

It didn't work.

She still felt miserable.

'If she was going to answer she'd have done it by now,' Pearl said gloomily.

For a sec she thought she saw a glint in Winston's eye.

The old glint he used to give her when he

thought she was being a pain in the guts.

Then she realised it was just the reflection of the frozen peas and sweet corn.

'Sorry to go on like this, Winston,' she said, removing a small icicle from his ear, 'but you're the only one I can talk to. None of the kids at school are speaking to me. Not since Craigette spread the rumour I'm a vampire.'

Pearl heard the front door bang.

She froze.

Mum was home.

'Pearl,' called Mum, 'what are you doing with your head in the freezer?'

Pearl quickly kissed Winston goodbye and slipped him under the bags of frozen peas and sweet corn.

She closed the freezer door just as Mum came in.

Pearl started to explain that she'd just been trying to cheer herself up, hoping that Mum would think she'd been looking for icypoles.

Then she saw Mum wasn't listening.

'... Howard couldn't believe it,' Mum was saying.

Couldn't believe what, thought Pearl, that some cages are called hutches?

'His mother announcing that she's coming down, just like that,' said Mum. 'She hasn't been down here for years.'

Pearl stared at Mum, heart thumping.

'She must have liked your letter, or whatever you sent her,' said Mum. 'She arrives on Saturday.'

Pearl struggled to control herself.

'So,' said Mum, 'you've got a babysitter. Look happy, if it's not too much effort.'

Pearl looked happy.

It wasn't any effort at all.

The effort was in stopping herself from flinging the freezer open, grabbing Winston and dancing round the house with him.

'Pearl,' shouted Mum, 'where's my red bra?'

Pearl sighed.

She stuck her head out of her room and yelled 'In the dryer'.

Then she went back to her Grandma Check List.

Rocking chair with comfy embroidered cushion.

Check.

Crocheted blanket with roses on it.

Pearl looked at the roses more closely and decided they were brussel sprouts.

Never mind.

Check.

Fluffy slippers.

Check.

China tea pot with matching cups and almost-matching saucers.

Check.

Pearl sighed happily.

It was everything a grandma could want.

She felt like running back down to the Salvation Army depot and hugging everyone there for giving all this stuff to a poor frail old woman they hadn't even met.

She didn't, because she couldn't take her eyes off the rocking chair.

It was perfect, even though the varnish was a bit chipped.

She imagined Grandma in it, blanket over her knees, fluffy slippers snug on her feet, sipping tea, her kind old face beaming at Pearl.

Pearl would sit at Grandma's feet and put her head on Grandma's lap and Grandma would stroke her hair.

They'd be sitting by the window in a ray of warm sunlight.

Not too warm, in case Winston melted.

'Pearl,' yelled Mum, 'the red bra was in the drawer. I can't trust you with anything.'

Pearl hadn't been to the airport since arriving in town two years earlier.

She'd forgotten how noisy it could get when there was a plane on the tarmac revving its

43

propellers.

'You watch out for Howard's mother while we check in,' shouted Mum, pushing Howard towards the counter. 'She's getting off the plane we're getting on.'

Pearl went and stood by the Arrivals/Departures door.

Her guts were scrabbling so fast and her heart was booming so loud she couldn't think straight.

This is ridiculous, she thought after a bit, I don't know what she looks like.

She decided to greet every kind-faced little old lady just in case.

Except none of the people coming through the door were kind-faced little old ladies.

Relax, Pearl said to herself. Frail old folk always wait till last to get off a plane so they can be helped down the steps.

She glanced over at the check-in counter to see if the airline had wheelchairs for really old and frail grandmas.

While Pearl's head was turned, a loud rasping noise echoed through the terminal. It sounded like one of the propellers had come off the plane and was skidding across the tarmac.

Towards her.

Pearl spun round.

The noise wasn't coming from skidding metal, it was coming from an elderly woman.

A broad-shouldered elderly woman with the sleeves of her dress rolled up and a large suitcase in each hand and a cigarette in her mouth which sprayed ash each time she coughed.

There was a skinny boy standing behind the woman, slapping her on the back. He was whacking her as hard as he could, but it didn't seem to be making much difference.

Poor bloke, thought Pearl, having a grandma like that. She wouldn't fit into fluffy slippers. She probably wouldn't even fit into a rocking chair. If she tried to stroke your hair she'd probably set it on fire.

The boy's grandma finally stopped coughing.

She put her suitcases down, adjusted her bosom and pushed the sleeves of her dress up over her biceps.

Then she grinned at Pearl.

'G'day,' she said, 'you must be Pearl. I'm Gran.'

They sat in the back of the taxi waiting for the driver to heave the bags into the boot.

Pearl tried not to look like she was sulking.

It wasn't easy.

Just my luck, she thought bitterly. Instead of a grandma I get a retired wrestler. Plus she brings her real grandkid with her so I won't even get a look in.

'Mitch was that excited on the plane,' said

Gran, 'I thought he was gunna poop himself.'

'Gran,' said Mitch, sounding embarrassed.

Pearl snuck a look at him round Gran's broad chest.

He was the thinnest kid she'd ever seen.

Pearl realised he was giving her a friendly grin.

At that moment Gran leant forward for a cough, so Pearl didn't have to grin back.

The driver got in and Pearl opened her mouth to tell him the address. Before she could, Gran slapped a big hand on the driver's shoulder.

'The lake,' she said.

She grinned at Pearl.

'Bit of sightseeing on the way.'

Pearl's guts tightened.

That's all I need, she thought. A grandma with no concept of how expensive taxis are.

'Mum only gave me five dollars,' she said.

Gran didn't hear.

She was squeezing one of Mitch's spindly knees.

'Only joshing,' she said to him. 'Sorry if I embarrassed you.'

Mitch grinned.

Gran grinned back and punched him in the shoulder.

Pearl sighed.

Chapter Six

Gran stood at the edge of the lake and stared out over the water.

'Hasn't changed a bit,' she said.

She stood lost in thought, puffing on a cigarette.

In the back of the taxi Pearl stared too.

At the meter.

Eleven dollars thirty.

She took a deep breath and wondered how she could get Gran and Mitch back in the cab.

Set fire to their suitcases?

From the look of Mitch he wouldn't care.

He was running excitedly through the lakeside mud and reeds towards a small beach.

When he reached it he pulled off most of his clothes and ran into the water.

'Hope he's got a towel,' said the driver, going back to his newspaper.

Pearl sighed and looked at the meter.

Eleven dollars fifty.

She wondered what the extra charge would be for dripping on a taxi seat.

Her calculation was interrupted by a loud rasping noise.

Gran was doubled over, coughing.

'Hope she's got a hanky,' said the driver, not looking up from his newspaper.

When Gran finally stopped coughing, the meter said twelve dollars twenty.

This is ridiculous, thought Pearl. At this rate we'll use up all the money Mum left for take-away and we'll have to survive on guinea pig grain.

She peered across the lake.

Mitch wasn't to be seen.

Must be seeing how long he can hold his breath under water, thought Pearl wearily. Won't be long, with his skinny lungs.

She waited.

Any second now he'd be popping up, blue in the face and gasping.

She waited some more.

Then she got out of the taxi, starting to feel uneasy.

'Gran,' she said.

Gran was gazing out over the water again.

Must be remembering the floods, thought Pearl. Probably wishing she'd had lino instead of carpet.

'Gran,' shouted Pearl.

Gran looked round.

Pearl pointed to Mitch's clothes on the beach.

Gran squinted at them.

Then she dropped her cigarette and dashed through the reeds.

Pearl ran after her.

'Mitch,' Gran was shouting. 'You can't swim, you stupid idiot.'

She doubled up with another coughing fit.

Pearl sprinted past her and without stopping to take off any clothes, dived in.

She could tell the water was deep because it was freezing.

She opened her eyes and waited for them to get used to the murkiness.

Suddenly she saw movement.

She couldn't tell how far away it was, or even what it was.

Something thrashing around.

Please, she thought, let it be Mitch's arms and legs.

And if not, an old rotary clothes hoist in a swarm of mullet rather than a giant octopus.

Teeth chattering, Pearl tried to swim over for a closer look, but each time she kicked her legs they snapped straight, jarring her whole body.

Something was wrapped round her ankles.

She pushed herself deeper to shake it off.

Slimy tendrils brushed her face and cut into her armpit.

Then she remembered.

Chest weed.

She'd heard people talking about it.

Winston had heard them too.

If he wasn't in the freezer he'd have reminded her before she dived in.

They called it chest weed because it wrapped itself round the chests of swimmers, and the ones that drowned ended up with it growing inside their ribcages.

Pearl tore at it but her fingers slipped off.

It was like slimy birthday present ribbon but a million times stronger.

OK, she said silently to the weed. I'll do a deal. Let me go and I'll be grateful for Gran.

The weed didn't budge.

She kicked as hard as she could and felt it cutting into her waist.

Her heart was scrabbling.

She was running out of breath.

Then suddenly the water exploded and there were bubbles surging all around her.

Pearl saw a huge dark shape moving towards her through the water.

A whale?

A fridge full of energetic fish?

No, it was Gran.

*

Gran wasn't the only one coughing as she dragged them into the shallows.

Pearl knelt in the muddy water and coughed harder than she ever had in her life.

She coughed up water, bits of weed, half her guts it felt like.

When they'd all stopped, Gran grabbed Mitch by the neck.

'You dopey mongrel,' she roared, 'you know you can't swim.'

'I'm learning,' croaked Mitch. 'I can't learn on dry land, can I?'

Gran spat disgustedly into the water.

She reached into the sodden folds of her dress and pulled out an even more sodden packet of cigarettes.

'I'm beginning to reckon,' she rasped, squeezing the packet into pulp, 'that perhaps I shouldn't have brung you.'

Mitch looked so hurt that Pearl felt a bit sorry for him.

Even though he was an idiot.

Then Gran sighed and gave him a grin.

'Only joshing,' she said.

She turned to Pearl.

'And you,' she said. 'In your letter you sounded a right tragic case. Now I get here and find you're a hero.'

Before Pearl could answer, Gran clamped her in a painfully tight hug.

Pearl struggled to explain that she wasn't a tragic case, just a bit lonely, but Gran was squeezing her too hard.

From the shore came a quiet cough.

Pearl looked up.

It was the taxi driver.

'Hope you've got some dry money,' he said.

When Pearl came out of her room with dry clothes on, Mitch was in the rocking chair rubbing his hair with a towel.

He looked at her sheepishly.

'Thanks for trying to save me.'

'S'OK,' said Pearl. 'I'd have done it for anyone. Well, maybe not Craigette Benson.'

Mitch grinned.

Don't grin, thought Pearl, you don't even know who Craigette Benson is.

'Why did you go out so deep if you can't swim?' she asked.

'It's a long story,' said Mitch.

She saw he was watching her closely.

'For most of my life,' he said, 'I've had a guardian angel.'

Pearl stared at him.

Perhaps her ears were blocked with chest weed and she hadn't heard him properly.

'Doug's invisible,' continued Mitch, 'but he keeps an eye on me and stops me getting hurt.'

Pearl rolled her eyes.

That's all she needed.

A loony cousin.

She waited for him to go on, possibly about his visits to Mars, but he was staring at the towel, picking at a thread.

'Doesn't matter,' he said.

Pearl wondered if there was some medicine she should be giving him.

Gran came out of the bathroom with a towel round her and a cigarette in her mouth and her hair spiked up.

'Ripper shower,' she said. 'Water up our way's so full of mineral salts it's like washing in gravel.'

Her feet were making puddles on the carpet.

Pearl thought about offering her the fluffy slippers.

Not much point.

She'd only fit a couple of toes in.

Gran blew out smoke and had a cough.

Perhaps she's got a dry throat, thought Pearl.

'Would you like a cup of tea?' she asked, pointing to the almost-matching china tea set on the coffee table next to Mitch.

'I'd rather have a beer,' said Gran, rummaging in one of her suitcases.

Gran pulled out a plastic thermos and poured herself a beaker of what looked to Pearl like the brown stuff that had come out of Winston's bottom the time he'd eaten too much mucsli.

'I have to guzzle this health sludge three times a day,' said Gran, taking a swig and grimacing. 'Yoghurt, bran, lecithin, kelp and some sort of pollen. Doc reckons it'll keep me healthy. It's pretty crook if I don't have something to wash it down.'

'Sorry,' said Pearl, feeling sick, 'Mum doesn't drink beer.'

'No worries,' said Gran, 'I'll pick up a slab later. Hey, top rocker.'

She went over to the rocking chair and stroked it admiringly.

Pearl took a deep breath.

'I got it for you,' she said quietly.

Gran beamed at her.

'That was very sweet Pearl, thank you.'

Mitch stood up.

'Be careful Gran,' he said. 'You don't want to hurt yourself like you did when you fell backwards off Geoff Nile's trail bike.'

Gran aimed a pretend swipe at him.

Then she licked her lips and rubbed her hands together.

'OK,' she said, 'let's give it a twirl.'

She squeezed herself into the chair and slowly

rocked back and forward, eyes closed, face glowing with pleasure.

'I could spend my last days in this little beauty,' she said, 'no risk.'

Pearl felt a grin creep across her own face.

She reached for the crocheted blanket.

Then, with a creak and a loud snap, the chair collapsed.

'Gran,' shouted Mitch.

Gran, speechless with astonishment, lay on her back among splintered wood and pieces of shattered tea set.

Then she roared with laughter.

Pearl stared, horrified.

Mitch started to laugh too.

Pearl ran into the kitchen.

She flung open the freezer door and stuck her head inside.

'It's a disaster, Winston,' she said. 'My only chance at a grandma and she's a monster.'

Pearl pressed Winston's frozen fur to her wet cheek.

'I don't know what we're going to do,' she whispered.

Winston's eye didn't glint.

He obviously didn't have any suggestions.

Chapter Seven

'Twenty-three minutes,' said Pearl indignantly.

She pressed her ear to the bedroom wall.

The shower was still running and Mitch was still singing the theme to 'Star Trek'.

'Twenty-three minutes he's been in there,' she said to Winston. 'Mum'll go spare when she gets back and sees the electricity bill.'

A tear rolled down Winston's cheek and plopped onto the bedspread.

Pearl picked him up anxiously.

'It's not that serious,' she said.

Then she realised it was just his ice melting.

'Come on,' she said sadly, 'better get you back to the freezer.'

She wrapped Winston in a clean T-shirt and hurried out into the hallway.

And stopped dead.

Gran was blocking the way.

Pearl could feel melting ice running down her arm.

She wished she'd wrapped Winston in something bigger.

A sheet or a raincoat.

Gran saw Pearl and smiled.

'Sorry his lordship's hogging the bathroom,' she said. 'We had a drought for eight years before the flood and he's never been in a shower that goes for longer than two minutes.'

Pearl clutched the T-shirt and desperately hoped she hadn't left any bits of Winston poking out.

Grans who broke rocking chairs and tea sets, even if they did pretend they were sorry later, weren't the sort of grans who'd understand about frozen guinea pigs.

Pearl had an awful vision of Winston in the garbage and Gran yelling about rodents.

Or even worse, in a casserole dish.

She'd heard about outback people. In droughts they ate anything that moved.

'Mitch,' yelled Gran. 'Out of that shower or I'll put a knot in the hot water pipe.'

Her eyesight must be going, thought Pearl gratefully. She hasn't even noticed I'm holding a soggy T-shirt.

Gran turned back to Pearl and pointed to the soggy T-shirt.

'When you've finished your washing,' she said, 'fancy giving me a hand? I've promised Mitch a swimming lesson this morning and I'm still feeling a bit tuckered out after our dip in the lake yesterday.'

Pearl desperately tried to think of an excuse. She couldn't.

All she could think of was getting Winston to the kitchen before he completely defrosted.

'OK,' she said.

'Good-o,' said Gran, and wheezed into Mum's bedroom.

Pearl hurried down the hall.

'Relax,' she whispered to the T-shirt. 'She didn't see you.'

Pearl stood in the shallow end of the pool and wished she was somewhere else.

Bed.

The movies.

The dentist.

She glanced over at the wooden bench outside the changing rooms.

Gran waved encouragingly.

Oh well, thought Pearl, let's get it over with.

'Watch closely what I do with my arms and legs,' she said to Mitch, 'then you try it.'

She swam across the pool, weaving through the other swimmers.

Mitch watched closely.

Then he tried it.

After two strokes he sank.

'OK,' said Pearl, after he'd surfaced spluttering, 'watch carefully how I float.'

She floated on her back for thirty seconds.

Mitch watched closely.

Then he tried it.

After two seconds he sank.

While he surfaced spluttering, Pearl took a weary breath.

The pool didn't close for another six hours.

'OK,' she said, 'I'll hold you.'

Mitch lay back onto the water and Pearl held him under his shoulders.

'Yes!' he shouted. 'I'm floating. Gran, look.'

Gran waved encouragingly.

'Let go,' yelled Mitch.

Pearl sighed and let go.

Mitch sank.

'Mitch,' said Pearl, after he'd surfaced spluttering, 'I'm not a very good swimming teacher. Gran'd be much better.'

'It's not your fault,' said Mitch, digging water out of his ear. 'I've got heavy bones. Dad's the same. You're doing a really good job.'

'Thanks,' said Pearl.

She wondered what a bad job would be. Holding him under and drowning him?

'Anyway,' said Mitch, 'Gran shouldn't go into swimming pools. She's got a bad chest.'

'She managed OK in the lake,' said Pearl.

She turned towards the bench to plead with Gran to take over.

Gran was talking to one of the pool attendants.

At last, thought Pearl, she's bringing in a professional.

Gran came to the edge of the pool.

'I'm feeling a bit tuckered out,' she said, 'so I'm going home for a health sludge and a lie down. This nice bloke'll keep an eye on you both. Oo-roo.'

The pool attendant waved encouragingly.

Pearl sighed.

Gran gave them a thumbs up and walked off.

Pearl turned back to Mitch.

'Why do you want to learn to swim anyway?' she asked. 'Where you live there's a drought most of the time.'

'And floods the rest of the time,' said Mitch. 'That's why I've decided to devote my life to flood control. Floods wreak terrible havoc on sheep and soft furnishings and families. My family's been torn apart by one. Mum and Dad sent me down here with Gran cause there's poo floating in our main street and they're too busy coordinating the clean-up committee to keep an eye on me. I want to find a way of harnessing the power of floods and using it for the good of humanity and livestock and families.'

Pearl stared at him.

His eyes were shining with excitement and chlorine.

'If you're going to control floods,' she said, 'why do you need to be able to swim?'

Mitch grinned.

'For when I make mistakes.'

Pearl found herself grinning too.

It was exactly the sort of thing Winston would say.

'Let's try backstroke,' said Mitch.

Pearl did backstroke across the pool.

Mitch watched closely.

Then he tried it.

After two metres he sank.

Exasperated, Pearl waited for him to surface spluttering.

'Mitch,' she said. 'This guardian angel you reckon you've got. Why don't you ask him to keep you afloat?'

Mitch's face dropped.

'He's not around any more. Guardian angels are for little kids, see, and he was spending too much time looking after me and I was really worried there'd be little kids missing out, so I told him to nick off.'

He bit his lip and stared at a four year old doing backstroke.

'I really miss him, but.'

Pearl realised she was biting her lip too.

This is ridiculous, she thought.

He's a total loony.

Off with the fairies.

A sandbag short of a flood control barrier.

So how come I know how he feels?

Pearl dumped her swimming bag on her bedroom floor and dumped herself down next to it.

I'm going to stay here for the rest of my life, she thought, and be a shoe rack.

At least it won't be as exhausting as being a swimming teacher.

She heard Mitch in the kitchen telling Gran that the swimming lesson had lasted more than three hours.

'So can you swim?' she heard Gran ask.

Pearl shook her head.

'How about float?' she heard Gran ask.

Pearl shook her head.

'He can sink,' she muttered.

Then she smelt something.

She dragged herself to her feet, sniffing frantically, panic clawing inside her.

She could smell cooked peas and sweet corn.

And something else she didn't recognise.

She sprinted to the kitchen, heart scrabbling.

Gran was at the stove, shovelling food from the wok onto plates.

'G'day,' said Gran. 'I've done a bit of a stir-fry for tea. Found a few things in the freezer.'

Pearl stared at the peas and corn and nearly fainted.

Mixed in with them were small strips of pale meat.

Chapter Eight

Pearl felt her blood go cold. Even colder than Winston's had been until recently.

Gran and Mitch were staring at her.

Then Gran started to laugh.

Even though the kitchen was spinning and Pearl felt like she was going to throw up, she still managed to calculate the number of years jail Gran would get for cooking a member of the family.

Twenty at least.

And an extra ten for laughing.

Then she realised Gran was shaking her and saying something.

'It's chicken,' Gran was shouting, eyes wet with mirth.

'Chicken?' Pearl heard herself say.

'Chicken,' said Gran.

Pearl flung open the freezer and rummaged

frantically through the apple pies and mini pizzas.

No Winston.

She turned back to Gran.

'If that's not Winston in the wok,' she demanded, 'where is he?'

Gran reached into the back of the freezer and opened a plastic salad crisper.

Inside lay Winston on a slice of bread.

Pearl felt relief flood through her.

'The ice was making his fur sodden,' said Gran, 'so I put him in there. The bread'll soak up the humidity and stop him going mouldy.'

She put a big sympathetic hand on Pearl's shoulder.

Shaking, Pearl picked up the crisper.

'We're feeling a bit tuckered out,' Pearl said with dignity, 'so we're going to our room for a lie down.'

Later, after Pearl's breathing was back to normal and she'd apologised to Winston for her relative's rudeness in making him move home without asking, there was a tap at her door.

Mitch poked his head in.

He was holding a plate of stir-fry.

'Do you want any?' he asked.

Pearl glared at him.

'Sorry,' he said, and went.

Pearl lay with Winston for a long time and

thought about a lot of things, including feral grans and mad cousins and becoming a vegetarian.

Later still, when Winston was starting to thaw, Pearl took him back to the freezer and tucked him in with a fresh slice of bread and said goodnight.

On her way back down the hall she heard a noise coming from Mum's room.

It sounded like more mirth.

Probably Gran still having a chuckle about my mistake, thought Pearl.

Then she realised it wasn't laughter.

It was sobbing.

The door was open a crack.

Pearl peered in.

Gran was sitting on the bed in a thick nightie, shoulders heaving, tears streaming.

Pearl stared, shocked.

Then she understood.

She tapped on the door, went in and put her hand on Gran's shoulder.

Gran looked up, startled.

'It's OK,' said Pearl. 'You don't have to be sad. Even though it was a tragedy Winston dying, he and I still have a pretty good relationship.'

She grabbed a handful of tissues from Mum's

bedside table and pushed them into Gran's hands.

Gran seemed confused.

Then she managed a small grin through her tears.

Phew, thought Pearl. Glad I spotted that. She might have been blubbing all night.

As Pearl watched Gran mop up with the tissues, she felt a small grin of her own bubble up inside her.

Who'd have guessed, she thought. A tough old chook like Gran getting upset over Winston.

For a fleeting second Pearl had a powerful urge.

She pushed it away.

Don't be a dope, she told herself.

Even when they are a bit soft-hearted and need cheering up, feral grans don't like kids trying to cuddle them.

Even later, just as Pearl was about to drop off, Gran came into her room.

'You asleep?' she whispered.

Fat chance of that, thought Pearl, with all the coughing you just did coming down the hall.

'Not quite,' she said.

'Want a chocolate crackle?' asked Gran.

Pearl sat up.

Gran, looming large in the light from the hallway, was holding a plate.

'I can't sleep sometimes,' said Gran, 'and a crackle or two seems to help.'

Trying not to smile, Pearl clicked on the bedside lamp and Gran sat on the bed.

'Dig in,' said Gran. 'Mind if I smoke?'

Pearl shook her head and took a bite of crackle.

It tasted a bit unusual.

'I put muesli in 'em,' said Gran through a mouthful, 'and a bit of kelp.'

Pearl decided she liked the taste.

'What's kelp?'

'Dried seaweed,' said Gran.

Pearl wished she hadn't asked.

But they still tasted OK.

'I like a bit of a midnight feast,' said Gran.

'Me too,' said Pearl.

She didn't mention it was the first time she'd ever had one with anybody over eleven.

'Should we invite Mitch?' she asked.

Please, she said silently, say no.

'No,' said Gran, 'I had one with him just before we left. More than one a week's not good for a kid.'

Pearl nodded happily to show she agreed and took another crackle.

'But,' said Gran, 'I hope you don't mind, I did bring fish.'

Pearl stared at her.

Fish?

With chocolate crackles?

'His actual name is Frank,' said Gran, 'but everyone calls him Fish cause he was a top swimmer.'

Pearl looked around the room.

'My husband,' said Gran. 'I couldn't bring him in person, of course, cause he died seven years ago.'

Pearl stared at Gran again.

She was starting to see where Mitch got being a loony from.

'How did you bring him then?' she asked cautiously.

Gran started laughing, and then choking on her crackle. Red in the face, she pointed over her shoulder.

For a scary sec Pearl thought she meant Fish was out in the hall.

Then she understood.

She whacked Gran on the back.

Gran had a coughing fit.

Bits of crackle pinged off Pearl's wardrobe.

'I saw what you were thinking,' wheezed Gran when she could finally speak. 'You were thinking I had a big freezer somewhere.'

Pearl nodded.

She hadn't been, but with this woman anything was possible.

Gran shook her head, then tapped it with her finger.

'He's in here,' she said. 'In my head. Not his actual body of course, cause then I'd have arms and legs sticking out my ears. But all the best bits of him. The bit of him, for example, that made him give up the chance to swim in the district championships cause I was having Howard's sister. The backflips he did down the main street when an Aussie swimmer won a gold medal at some Olympics. Millions of bits.'

Pearl smiled.

If I'd been Howard, she thought, with a dad like that, I wouldn't have wasted time at the boring old opera.

'I invite the old bloke to lots of things,' said Gran. 'Just like you probably invite Winston to lots of things.'

Pearl grinned and went to jump out of bed.

'Yeah,' she said, 'Good idea. I'll get him.'

Gran held Pearl's arm.

'I don't mean that poor frozen old carcass out there,' she said quietly. 'I mean the real Winston.'

Pearl was speechless.

Poor frozen old carcass?

'That is the real Winston,' she said indignantly. 'I should know, I . . .'

Gran was tapping her on the head.

'The best bits,' said Gran. 'What was the funniest thing he ever did?'

'Well ...' said Pearl doubtfully, 'one was when Mum had some clients to dinner and they were still here really late and making a lot of noise and Winston got over-tired and went into the bedroom where their coats were and tried to have sex with a fur jacket.'

Gran roared with laughter, then had a coughing fit.

Pearl whacked her on the back.

Bits of crackle pinged around the room.

'And what was the kindest thing?' spluttered Gran.

'The night Dad left,' said Pearl quietly. 'Winston came into bed without me asking him to and slept really close to my face and soaked up quite a lot of the tears.'

Gran nodded thoughtfully.

Then she told Pearl some more of Fish's best bits and Pearl told her lots more of Winston's and there was a fair amount of coughing and whacking.

'I'll never forget Fish's funeral,' said Gran, munching her half of the last crackle. 'He wanted his ashes scattered in his beloved municipal swimming pool, so we did. Trouble was, it was empty cause of the drought and the council cleaners swept it out the next day.'

Pearl stared, horrified.

Gran grinned.

'Don't reckon it mattered to him that much,' she said. 'He ended up on the tip and he always liked the view from there. Didn't matter to me cause I had all the bits of him I wanted up here.'

Gran tapped her head again.

'You planning to have a funeral for Winston?' she asked.

Pearl didn't answer.

'Let me know if you are,' said Gran. 'I'm pretty hot at organising funerals.'

Suddenly Pearl felt very tired.

She turned off the bedside lamp.

'I think we should stop now,' she said. 'Good night.'

Chapter Nine

Pearl knew it was a dream, but it was still scary.

She and Winston were in the backyard watching Gran dig a hole with a big plastic spade.

At first Pearl thought it was going to be a swimming pool for Mitch.

Then the fruit shop van delivered a coffin.

Gran started complaining that the digging was making her fluffy slippers dirty and asked Pearl to take over.

'No!' screamed Pearl and woke up.

She could hear what sounded like a loud motor.

Oh no, she thought, Gran's got a mechanical digger.

Then she realised it was the blender.

Pearl staggered out to the kitchen.

Gran was standing at the sink pouring lumpy

brown goo from the blender into a glass.

'Want some health sludge?' she asked.

Pearl shuddered.

'No thanks,' she said, and hurried over to the freezer.

Winston was still lying on his slice of bread.

Pearl reached in and wiped some of the ice off his fur. She noticed that one of his ears was bent round at an angle. Carefully she straightened it.

It snapped off in her hand.

Pearl stared at it, horrified.

'Oh no,' she gasped. 'Winston, I'm sorry . . .'

'He didn't feel a thing,' said Gran softly, taking the ear from Pearl. 'Trust me.'

She dipped the edge of the ear into her glass of health sludge and stuck it back on Winston's head.

Then she closed the freezer door and leant against it.

Pearl wanted to push her out the way and run back to her room with Winston and hug him for hours.

Except she was terrified other bits might snap off.

'I've decided,' said Gran, 'that today's the day for getting rid of junk.'

Pearl got ready to wrestle Gran.

No way was she going to let Winston fall into

the clutches of a woman who reckoned he was junk.

'I've got some stuff stored over at Howard's place I haven't had a squiz at for a million years,' said Gran. 'Want to give me a hand?'

Pearl digested this.

Mitch wandered in, rubbing his hair with a towel.

'Today's a school day,' said Pearl. 'I've got to be there in twenty-five minutes.'

Gran swigged the health sludge.

'School'll be there tomorrow,' she said. 'How often does your Gran come to visit?'

'That's right,' grinned Mitch.

Pearl thought about Craigette Benson and the hilarious vampire graffiti she was probably scrawling in the girls' toilet at that moment.

I can't even take Winston to school to keep me company, thought Pearl. Not till his ear sets.

She looked at Gran.

'OK,' she said, 'but we're not going anywhere near the pet cemetery.'

It was a struggle, but finally they got the trapdoor open in the ceiling of Howard's spare bedroom and climbed into his roof cavity.

'Only tread on the beams,' wheezed Gran, 'or you'll fall through the ceiling and give Howard airconditioning he won't really want.'

Gran led the way along a beam through the dusty gloom.

Pearl felt cobwebs drag against her hair.

She sighed.

'Never a dull moment with Gran, eh?' whispered Mitch.

Don't know why he's so cheerful, thought Pearl gloomily. Doesn't he realise grans are meant to be dull? Dull and small and neat and cuddly with a strong preference for tea and scones and flower arranging rather than beer and chocolate crackles and funerals.

'Poop,' said Gran, and rubbed her head where she'd banged it on a roof support.

Pearl wondered if Gran banged her head much.

It would account for some of her behaviour.

'Hey-up,' said Gran. 'Here's the go.'

She was shining her torch at a pile of old wooden boxes.

Pearl did the same.

Spilling out of the boxes were dusty old toys, books, clothes, shoes and tyre inner tubes.

'Righto,' said Gran. 'Let's get all this shifted down and then we'll get a taxi to the tip.'

Pearl grabbed a box, then had a thought.

'Instead of dumping all this,' she said, 'why don't we give it to the Salvation Army. They fix this sort of stuff up and give it to kids.'

'OK,' said Gran. 'Good thought.'

They started dragging the boxes back along the beams.

Pearl had another thought.

'We should sort through it first,' she said. 'There might be some stuff you want to keep.'

'It's all going,' wheezed Gran.

Boy, thought Pearl, some people really don't want to remember their childhoods.

She wondered if she'd feel that way when she was ancient.

She had a sinking feeling she already did, so she made herself think about something else.

The tyre inner tubes were sticking out of her box. Now she was close to them, she wasn't sure if they were inner tubes. They were too small and fat and pink.

Pearl picked one up and realised what it was.

'Gran,' she said, 'are these floaties yours?'

Gran peered through the gloom.

'They're called water wings,' she said. 'Put them back.'

Pearl dragged the other one out.

'They're just what Mitch needs,' she said. 'Even he could float with these on.'

'Ripper,' said Mitch.

'No,' said Gran.

She snatched the water wings out of Pearl's hands.

At first Pearl assumed Gran was just being safety conscious. The rubber was cracking a bit in places.

Then she saw Gran's expression.

Pearl had never seen so much sadness on one face.

Not even on Winston's the night Dad left.

Gran's face was so creased Pearl was worried it would start cracking too.

Gran stared at the water wings for ages.

Then suddenly she bent forward into the torchlight and stuffed them angrily into her box of junk.

Her eyes, Pearl saw, were full of tears.

Pearl had never seen anyone drink beer so fast.

Three cans, gulp, gulp, gulp.

'It was the dust,' said Gran, wiping her mouth on the sleeve of her dress. 'That Salvo depot was almost as dusty as Howard's roof cavity.'

Then she went for a lie down.

Pearl went to see Mitch.

'Mitch,' she said, peering through the steam. 'can I have a word?'

'Do you mind,' squeaked Mitch. 'I'm in the shower!'

He tried to cover himself with the shampoo bottle.

'It's OK,' said Pearl, 'we're cousins.'

Mitch frantically tried to wrap himself in the shower curtain one-handed.

'Listen,' said Pearl. 'Why was Gran so upset about those water wings?'

'Dunno,' squeaked Mitch. 'Perhaps she was wishing she'd looked after them better. Now rack off.'

Pearl asked Winston what he thought.

Winston didn't seem that interested.

Not so much as a glint.

Then Pearl saw why.

His whiskers had fallen off.

'You poor thing,' she said. 'Here am I pestering you with other people's problems and you're suffering from terminal frostbite.'

She turned the temperature in the freezer down a bit and put another couple of slices of bread into his crisper.

But even while she was worrying about Winston, and wondering if he'd be better off in aluminium foil, she still couldn't forget about the water wings and that look on Gran's face.

Gran was lying on the bed in a cloud of smoke.

'Gran,' said Pearl, after she'd tapped on the door and crept in, 'can I tell you something?'

Gran stared at the ceiling and didn't answer.

I think that's probably a yes, thought Pearl.

'I just wanted to let you know that you don't

have to be too upset about your water wings being a bit perished cause the sports store in the main street sells them. I rang up and checked. They're plastic, not rubber and they're twenty-nine ninety-five.'

Gran didn't say anything for a while.

Then she blew smoke out so hard it almost reached the ceiling.

Oh dear, thought Pearl. They're too expensive.

Gran turned and looked at her with sad eyes.

It's a problem for old people, thought Pearl. They can't keep up with the cost of things.

'Is that why you were upset?' asked Pearl quietly.

Gran's big hand flew out and grabbed Pearl's arm.

Tight.

'I'm sixty-eight years old,' said Gran, 'and I've known you three days. Something you'll learn, young lady, is that people don't spill their guts about everything to people they've known three days.'

Pearl's heart was pounding and her arm was hurting.

She felt her eyes getting hot.

'Personal,' said Gran. 'Do you know what that means?'

Pearl nodded miserably.

'Good,' said Gran quietly, letting go of Pearl's arm. 'Now hop it.'

Pearl fled.

She threw herself down in her room.

OK Gran, she thought bitterly, have it your way. I won't ever care about you again.

Ever.

Then she realised something was digging into her face.

Something on the carpet.

She peered at it.

It was a piece of chocolate crackle.

Pearl sat up.

Oh no you don't Gran, she thought.

You're the only Gran I've got and you're not getting rid of me that easily.

I'm going to find out about those dumb water wings if it kills me.

Chapter Ten

Pearl's feet were killing her.

I bet I've never walked this far in my life, she thought wearily.

Nearly there.

She could see the old people's home at the top of the hill.

Keep going, she told herself. This is normal. You can't expect to solve a mystery without a bit of leg pain. If you stop for a rest now your legs'll go completely stiff and there probably isn't a vacant wheelchair for miles around.

She trudged on.

To take her mind off the stabbing pains, she added up the total distance she'd walked so far.

From the house to the Salvos depot must have been about one kilometre, though she'd used two kilometres of energy by running all the way in case someone else was in the middle of asking for the water wings.

Bursting into the shop and finding nobody was and getting them herself and flopping down on the kerb weak with relief had taken a bit of energy too.

But then spotting a name written on the water wings in faded ink and struggling to read the dodgy handwriting and finally working out it said Babs Cuncliffe had at least given her legs a rest.

From the Salvos to the post office must have been about half a kilometre.

Looking for a B Cuncliffe in the phone book and not finding one hadn't been a rest because she'd had to do it standing up.

From the post office to the cemetery had been another half a kilometre.

Walking around not finding a gravestone with Babs Cuncliffe on it had probably been two kilometres, not counting losing her temper and kicking a marble slab and hopping about for a bit.

From the cemetery to the Tobacco Co-op had been at least one-and-a-half kilometres.

Just as well she'd been able to have a long rest when she got there while Mum's secretary made a few enquiries in her capacity as vice-president of the Historical Society.

Because when Mum's secretary hung up the phone, she'd told Pearl that Miss Cuncliffe was living under her married name of Mrs Meadows in the Sunnyview Nursing Home near the airport.

Mum's office to the airport was four kilometres.

Which made the total for the day nine-and-a-half kilometres.

Pearl groaned again as she dragged herself up the nursing home driveway.

If Mrs Meadows can't solve the mystery of these dumb water wings, she thought, wincing with pain, I think I'll just check myself in and stay here till I'm old.

'Mrs Meadows?' said the woman in the office. 'She'll be delighted. She hasn't had a visitor all week. Come this way.'

Pearl followed the woman along a corridor that smelt almost as strong as the bathroom after Howard dropped Mum's cologne.

As they passed an open doorway, Pearl peeked in.

A very old man was lying on a bed surrounded by medical equipment with about six tubes connected to him.

Through a window he had a view of the airport.

Pearl shuddered.

Poor thing, she thought. He looks like he's being refuelled for take-off.

The office woman stopped outside a door, tapped on it, sang out 'Visitor, Mrs Meadows', pushed open the door, smiled at Pearl and hurried away.

Pearl held her breath and stepped into the room.

And stopped.

And stared.

Sitting up in bed smiling at her was the most perfect grandma she'd ever seen.

'Hello,' said Mrs Meadows, fluffing her curly grey hair and smoothing her lilac knitted bed-jacket and twinkling at Pearl with soft friendly eyes. 'What a lovely surprise.'

'Hello,' said Pearl, heart scrabbling.

They introduced themselves.

Mrs Meadows patted the bed.

'Come and sit down,' she smiled, 'and have some butter shortcake.'

Pearl did.

Boy, thought Pearl, they're lucky, whoever's got her for a grandma. Wonder if she's got any single sons about Mum's age?

Mrs Meadows patted Pearl's hand.

'You're a very kind girl,' said Mrs Meadows, 'to visit an old lady like me.'

Pearl glowed.

'I've brought something for you,' she said, digging into her jeans pockets.

Mrs Meadows twinkled with anticipation.

Pearl couldn't wait to see Mrs Meadows' face light up even more when she saw her pink rubber tubes from so long ago.

She handed Mrs Meadows the water wings.

Mrs Meadows looked at them for a long time.

Hope she doesn't get too emotional, thought Pearl. It's probably not good for a frail old soul like her.

Pearl watched anxiously.

Mrs Meadows didn't seem to be getting too emotional.

If anything, she was twinkling less.

She was even frowning a bit.

'Where did you get these?' she asked.

'I was helping my Gran clear some stuff out this morning,' said Pearl.

Mrs Meadows' face twisted into a snarl.

She threw the water wings at Pearl.

They bounced off Pearl's head and skidded across the floor.

'Flo Siberry?' spat Mrs Meadows. 'Flo Siberry's your Gran?'

Pearl sat stunned.

She forced her dazed brain into action.

Howard's name was Elyard, which must be

Gran's married name. Siberry must be her maiden name.

'Your Gran,' hissed Mrs Meadows, sticking her angry glaring face close to Pearl's, 'killed my brother.'

Pearl gaped.

She slid off the bed and backed away.

The room was starting to wobble.

It's not possible, she thought. Gran's been flat out ever since she got here. She hasn't had time to kill anyone.

'She was fifteen when she did it,' growled Mrs Meadows. 'My brother was seventeen. He'd fallen in love with her, God knows why. Went round telling everyone she was going to be the Tobacco Carnival Queen of 1947 or whenever it was. She didn't stand a chance. She was too tall and she had a face like a boot.'

Maybe he told Gran that, thought Pearl wildly, and that's why she killed him.

'In those days,' continued Mrs Meadows bitterly, 'carnival queens had to do more than just wobble their bits. They had to be citizens and sportswomen. Flo Siberry couldn't even swim, so she asked my brother to teach her.'

Mrs Meadows' chin was trembling.

She wiped her nose on the sleeve of her bedjacket.

'He took my water wings,' she said, 'without

asking, and he and your gran snuck off to the lake together and he drowned.'

Pearl felt weak with relief.

An accident.

Gran wasn't a murderer.

Then she thought about what it must have been like for Gran.

Seeing her boyfriend drown.

Poor thing.

Pearl realised Mrs Meadows' chin was trembling again.

'I'm really sorry,' Pearl said.

Mrs Meadows didn't answer.

Pearl swallowed.

What else could she say?

'What was your brother's name?' she asked quietly.

Mrs Meadows glowered at Pearl.

'I never say his name,' she said. 'I never even think it.'

She opened a bedside drawer and took out a book. Opening it, she held up the bookmark.

Pearl saw what it was.

A wisp of hair.

'That's all I've got left of my brother,' hissed Mrs Meadows. 'That's all your grandmother left me.'

Pearl watched as Mrs Meadows pressed the hair angrily to her lips.

You poor thing, she thought. You've hung onto the wrong bit.

By the time Pearl got home her head was aching almost as much as her feet.

First I'll have a lie down, she thought wearily on the doorstep, and then I'll have a quiet chat with Gran.

'It was a disaster,' said a loud voice inside, 'an absolute disaster.'

Mum's voice.

Pearl took a deep breath and went in.

Mum and Howard and Gran and Mitch were having dinner.

Pearl hadn't realised it was that late.

'Hello,' she said.

They all said hello. Gran gave her arm a gentle squeeze.

'You're late home from school,' said Mum. 'I was just telling Mrs Elyard, the trip was a disaster. We found a soapie actress but she pulled out at the last minute. So it's back to local talent if they can keep their cars away from power poles.'

Gran put a plate in front of Pearl.

'Mrs Elyard has cooked us a wonderful dinner,' said Mum. 'Stir-fried lamb with some wonderful herbs. What are they, Flo?'

'Just chilli,' said Gran, 'and some basil from the

herb tub outside.'

Mum stopped chewing and ran for the bathroom.

While Howard put Mum to bed and gave her some indigestion tablets, Pearl had a long talk with Winston in the freezer.

She explained to him how she didn't want to end up like Mrs Meadows.

She could see he understood.

Then she went out to the front yard.

Mitch was in the street with the hose, watering the nature strip.

Gran was sitting on her suitcases having a smoke and staring at the stars.

'I'm gunna be staying over at Howard's,' she said. 'Just for a bit.'

Pearl took a deep breath.

'I want to have a funeral for Winston,' she said quietly.

Gran stood up slowly and looked at Pearl.

'I was hoping you would,' she said. 'That's why I saved these.'

She opened her suitcase and showed Pearl the pieces of broken rocking chair wrapped in her nightie.

'I don't understand,' said Pearl.

'From what I hear,' said Gran, 'Winston was a pretty special individual. I reckon he deserves a pretty special funeral. The Vikings, those ancient warriors from up north, when they were giving their heroes a send-off, they used to put 'em in a boat and send 'em out across the water in glorious flames.'

Pearl grinned.

A Viking funeral.

That sounded like Winston.

Gran rubbed her chin and looked at the pieces of wood.

'Hope we can build a boat from these that'll float.'

'These might help,' said Pearl, digging into her pockets.

She handed Gran the water wings.

Gran looked at her for a bit, then grinned.

Pearl was tempted to say more, but she decided not to.

Gran had made it pretty clear that some things were personal.

When they got to the lake, dawn was just starting to break.

'Hope you've got a torch,' said the taxi driver, reaching for his paper.

They carried the Viking ship with Winston in it down to the water's edge.

This time Pearl didn't say goodbye too quickly.

She didn't say goodbye at all.

91

She stroked Winston's fur, so dry and soft after she and Gran had blow-dried it, and explained some stuff.

How he mustn't be alarmed when he found he didn't have a body anymore.

How he'd find being inside her head much nicer than being inside a freezer.

How she'd always love him.

When she'd finished holding him to her lips, she laid him on the nest of twigs and leaves inside the boat.

Together, Pearl and Gran pushed the boat out onto the silver water.

For a few minutes they watched it slowly drift away, silhouetted against the pink dawn.

Then Gran squirted lighter fluid onto a twig and ignited it and hurled the flaming stick in a high arc.

It landed in the boat.

'I used to be good at darts,' said Gran.

Soon the boat was ablaze, moving out towards the centre of the lake.

Gran and Pearl sat down to watch it.

When Pearl's tears came, she laid her head in Gran's lap.

After a while she realised she wasn't the only one crying.

She squeezed Gran's hand.

Much later, when the last burning piece of

wood had slipped beneath the surface of the lake, and Pearl had thought up the best idea she'd ever had in her whole life, Gran was still stroking her hair.

Chapter Eleven

Mum and the rest of the Carnival Queen Selection Committee were pretty surprised when they yelled 'next' and Pearl and Gran walked in.

Pearl could tell they were surprised because their mouths were hanging open.

She waited for them to recover.

Mum was first.

'Pearl,' she hissed angrily, leaping to her feet, 'what are you doing here?'

The rest of the people round the boardroom table started to chuckle.

'Sorry, lovey,' said Mr Tucker, the president of the Tobacco Growers Association, to Pearl. 'You've got to be over fifteen to be Carnival Queen.'

'Bring her back in a few years,' said Mr Longbeach, the chairman of the Co-op board, to

Gran. 'When she's got all her teeth.'

Pearl opened her mouth to explain.

'No argument please, young lady,' said Mum, steering them towards the door. 'We're very busy here and you're not over fifteen.'

Pearl pointed to Gran.

'She is.'

Gran nodded. 'And I've got all my teeth,' she said.

Mum hesitated, confused.

Pearl pulled herself free and faced the committee.

'Tobacco's been keeping this town going for seventy years,' she said. 'It's been keeping Gran going almost as long.'

Pearl watched the committee take this in.

She could hear Gran wheezing quietly behind her.

Don't cough, Pearl pleaded silently, please don't cough.

'Tobacco growing,' she continued to the committee, 'is a traditional part of this town. Well, so's Gran. She was born here sixty-eight years ago. I reckon we should have a Carnival Queen who represents our proud traditions and ancient heritage and all the stuff that's made this town great.'

Pearl stopped, out of breath.

Gran smiled winningly at the committee.

The committee smiled nervously back.

Pearl saw that Mum's secretary, representing the Historical Society, was applauding silently at the rear of the room.

'Pearl,' said Mum, voice low with angry exasperation, 'I thought I told you to check your hare-brained ideas with me first.'

Pearl looked pleadingly at the committee.

'You know,' said Mr Longbeach thoughtfully, 'the lassie does have a point.'

Pearl was surprised they said yes so quickly.

Forty-five minutes, she thought happily, including hugging and handshaking time.

Not bad for a committee.

Mum sometimes complained that committees took three hours just to decide what biscuits they wanted.

After tea and biscuits (chocolate fingers) with only a small amount of coughing from Gran and no crumbs pinging off the boardroom walls, Mum led everyone out the back to the storage area.

'This,' said Mr Tucker, 'is it.'

Gran squeezed Pearl's arm excitedly as they looked up at a huge throne covered in gold-sprayed tobacco leaves.

'There's a matching canopy,' said Mr Tucker,

'and a couple of Nubian slaves'll be fanning you with big matching fans. I say Nubian, it'll actually be Ron and Les Piggott with boot polish on.'

'Sounds tops,' said Gran happily.

'The whole thing goes on the back of a semi-trailer,' said Mum, 'and you'll be up there for a good couple of hours. Will you be able to cope with that?'

'I'm stronger than I look,' said Gran.

She put her arm round Mr Tucker's waist and lifted him off the ground.

Everyone laughed.

Except Pearl.

Don't overdo it Gran, begged Pearl silently. Tobacco Queens aren't meant to have coughing fits.

Gran put Mr Tucker down and had a coughing fit.

Everyone thought she was putting it on and laughed even louder.

'One last thing,' said Mr Longbeach to Gran. 'You are sympathetic, I assume, to the nature of our industry.'

'You mean do I think tobacco growing's a good idea?' said Gran. 'Anyone got a smoke?'

When they got back to Howard's place, Gran put her arms round Pearl.

'Thanks,' she said quietly. 'You don't know what a ripper this is for me.'

I think I do, thought Pearl happily.

They stood for a moment, Gran holding Pearl's head against her chest.

With her ear pressed to Gran's dress, Pearl could hear that each of Gran's breaths was a wheeze.

Oh no, she thought. I hope Gran didn't get pneumonia yesterday sitting by the lake all that time.

Then she remembered reading that people with pneumonia also have temperatures and clammy skin and splitting headaches.

Phew.

Gran went off to get dinner on and Mum came in from the car.

'Howard's off tranquillising a horse,' said Mum. 'When he gets back, he and I have got a business dinner.'

Pearl nodded.

She could see there was something else Mum wanted to say.

'Sorry I grouched at you back there,' said Mum. 'Your heritage idea was a pretty good one actually. Certainly saved me a few headaches.'

She rummaged in her bag.

'I was too busy to get you a prezzie in Sydney,' she said, 'so get yourself something, OK?'

Pearl stared at the fifty-dollar note Mum had stuffed into her hand.

Boy, she thought sadly, Mum must be feeling really guilty.

'Thanks,' she said.

Don't feel guilty Mum, she thought. There's no need. I've got a gran to look after me.

After Mum had gone to make a phone call, Pearl went to find Mitch to tell him the good news about Gran and the carnival.

He wasn't in his room.

Then Pearl noticed the trapdoor in the ceiling was open.

She climbed up into the roof cavity.

Mitch was sitting on a beam in the gloom.

'You OK?' asked Pearl.

'I can't stop thinking about that poor bloke you told me about,' said Mitch. 'Gran's boyfriend who drowned. If only he'd had a guardian angel, he'd have been right.'

'Perhaps he did,' said Pearl. 'Perhaps it all happened so quickly he didn't have a chance to call his guardian angel.'

'Or perhaps,' said Mitch gloomily, 'he'd sent his guardian angel away to look after little kids.'

Pearl looked at Mitch's sad freckled face and wished there was something she could do to help him feel better.

She realised there was.

Later, after she'd told her idea to Mitch and he'd got excited, she ran through it in her head with Winston.

He thought it was good idea, too.

'I can't take all the credit,' said Pearl modestly. 'I reckon having a Gran helps a person think better.'

The new water wings were bright yellow.

Pearl felt a bit embarrassed putting them on because it was after six and the swimming club people were training in the pool.

She put them on anyway.

No point buying them for Mitch and not showing him how to use them.

She showed him how they worked much better for breaststroke than crawl, and how for backstroke they were suicide.

'Let me try,' said Mitch excitedly.

He sat on the side and Pearl helped him put a pair on his arms and the other pair on his legs.

The man in the sports shop had told her she'd only need one pair, but she'd told the man in the sports shop he didn't know Mitch.

He must have understood because he'd let her have both pairs for fifty dollars.

'Today,' said Pearl, when Mitch was ready to go, 'just stretch out your arms and legs and float.'

Mitch slipped into the water.

He thrashed around for a while with only his arms and legs above the surface.

Pearl wondered if he was going to be the first person in the history of the world to drown with four water wings on.

Then, suddenly, Mitch was on his back with his arms and legs straight out and nearly half his body out of the water.

'I'm floating!' he yelled.

The swimming club people all looked over and joined Pearl in the applause.

Mitch didn't care.

He stayed floating for a long time, face dreamy.

Then he kicked himself to the side and took the water wings off.

'I can do it without the wings now,' he said, 'I know I can.'

'Are you sure?' said Pearl doubtfully.

'Yes,' said Mitch.

He lay slowly back in the water, and sank.

As she came into the house, Pearl sniffed expectantly for dinner.

Nothing.

Must be the chlorine up my nose, she thought. Gran's probably up to her elbows in stir-fry in the kitchen at this very moment.

Pearl went into Howard's big kitchen.

Gran wasn't at the stove, she was sitting at the table and she looked terrible.

Her face was grey and her shoulders were slumped.

Pearl stared at her in alarm.

Then Pearl saw that Mum and Howard were standing up the other end of the table.

Mum was staring at Gran too.

Not in alarm, in exasperation.

'Is this true?' said Mum to Gran.

Slowly, Gran nodded.

Howard put his head into his hands.

What's going on, thought Pearl. What's wrong?

None of them had seen her.

'If you knew this,' said Mum to Gran, her voice sounding strange, 'what on earth possessed you to think you could be Carnival Queen?'

Before Gran could answer, Mitch burst into the kitchen waving the water wings.

'I can float,' he yelled. 'Pearl got me these and I can float. Let's put a pool next to your throne, Gran, and I can float on the float.'

There was a long silence while everyone looked at everyone else.

'What is it?' said Pearl at last.

'Mrs Elyard isn't going to be Carnival Queen,' said Mum quietly.

'Why not?' said Pearl.

She wanted to shout it.

There was another silence.

Mum bit her lip.

'Tell them,' said Gran.

'Doctor Unwin was at our dinner,' said Mum, looking at the fridge, 'and he told Howard something he thought Howard should know about his mother. How she'd been to his surgery this afternoon.'

Pearl stared anxiously at Gran.

Gran stared miserably at the kitchen table.

Oh no, thought Pearl. You poor thing. You have got pneumonia. Or at least a bad chest cold.

'Mrs Elyard asked the doctor for pain-killing drugs,' continued Mum. 'Because ... because ...'

Pearl's heart started scrabbling.

Mum was never lost for words.

'Because,' said Gran quietly, 'I've got lung cancer.'

Chapter Twelve

Pearl lost track of time.

People were talking, but she wasn't sure if it was for minutes or hours.

Gran seemed to be doing quite a bit of it.

About the flood up her way.

About the trip she made to the city with some of the other flooded-out people in an army plane.

About the medical tests she had done on the quiet while she was there.

About the doctor who told her she had lung cancer.

About the specialist who told her it was too far gone to be cured.

Then Mitch started crying and Howard started shouting about why hadn't Gran told people.

Dimly, Pearl heard Gran say 'I didn't want to upset everyone.'

Howard and Mum got upset and told her that was ridiculous.

They started talking about hospitals in Sydney and second opinions, but Pearl didn't follow much of what they were saying.

Because suddenly her mind was racing.

Suddenly she knew what had to happen.

'Wait!' she shouted.

The others stopped talking and stared at her.

'Why can't Gran still be Carnival Queen?' she said.

Mum took a very big breath and snatched Gran's cigarettes off the table.

'Because,' she said, 'the Tobacco Carnival is to celebrate the growing of, surprise, surprise, tobacco.'

She thrust the packet of cigarettes in Pearl's face.

Pearl read the words printed on it.

SMOKING CAUSES LUNG CANCER

'Exactly,' Pearl shouted. 'Everyone knows that. So why can't Gran still be Carnival Queen?'

Pearl lay on the floor, furious.

Why is it, she thought bitterly, that whenever there's an argument between grown-ups and kids, the grown-ups always send the kids to their rooms?

And if their rooms aren't available, to other people's rooms?

Pearl looked around Mitch's bedroom.

There wasn't even a Winston-sized cushion, so she couldn't even have a decent cry.

She could hear Mum and Howard out in the living room, Howard on the phone and Mum on her mobile, yelling at doctors and specialists and hospitals in Sydney.

On the bed Mitch blew his nose on the sheet.

'It's more important she get cured,' he said, 'than be in some dopey carnival.'

Pearl sat up.

If Mitch hadn't been looking so sad and waterlogged, she'd have given him a shake.

'That's the whole point,' she said. 'Being Carnival Queen could cure her. It'll lift her spirits. Give her lungs the strength to fight back.'

Mitch stared at her.

'You're mental,' he said. 'If being a carnival queen cured lung cancer, there'd be thousands of carnivals every day with busloads of queens.'

Pearl sighed.

Cousins could be real dopes sometimes.

'It only works,' she said, 'for people who've been dreaming of being one for fifty-three years.'

There was a tap on the door.

Gran came in.

She gave each of them a long hug.

'I'm sorry,' she said, 'for not spilling the beans earlier.'

'Some things are personal,' said Pearl quietly.

'Mitch,' said Gran, 'thanks for coming all this way with me. It's a real tonic having you around. Took some sweat to persuade your mum and dad to let you come, but I'm glad they did.'

Pearl watched as Mitch digested this.

'And Pearl,' said Gran, 'thanks for writing that letter and reminding me I had a home town and some stuff to do here.'

Pearl realised with a stab of panic that Gran seemed to be making some sort of farewell speech.

Gran put her arms round them both.

'I'm sorry,' she said, 'that I can't be your Gran for a whole lot longer, but that's the way the crackle crumbles.'

'Gran,' said Pearl fiercely, 'don't give up.'

'I've sent a message to Doug,' said Mitch. 'It might take a while to get to him, but as soon as he picks it up he'll be here to help cure you, I know.'

Gran sighed.

It came out as a wheeze.

'You're both champs,' she said.

'Gran,' said Pearl, 'if you could still be Carnival Queen, would you?'

Gran gave a tired grin.

'Course I would,' she said. 'But I know that's off the bookie's sheet now, and that's OK, it was a lovely thought. So instead I'm going outside for a smoke.'

Pearl stared at Gran.

She felt like ringing up the cigarette companies and telling them to put another notice on their packets.

SMOKING MAKES LUNG CANCER WORSE

Gran must have read her mind.

She gave another weary grin.

'I'm gunna die anyway,' she said, 'eh?'

Not if I can help it, thought Pearl.

Mr Benson finished tying a cauliflower to his bullbar and shook his head.

'Sorry,' he said, 'but by the time I've got all the produce on the back of the truck, and Craigette in her spinach costume, there won't be room for another person.'

'See,' said Craigette. 'I told you.'

Pearl resisted the temptation to dress Craigette for the carnival a day early with rotten tomatoes.

'Please Mr Benson,' she said, 'you could be saving an old lady's life.'

Mr Benson sighed.

'She wouldn't feel comfortable,' he said, tying a bunch of carrots to his rear vision mirror. 'The theme of the truck this year is spring vegies, which is why I'm going to the expense of doing Craigette in baby spinach rather than silver beet.

Wouldn't really work with an elderly person on board, eh?'

'See?' said Craigette.

The manager of Foley's Trucking and Haulage (A'asia) Pty Ltd finished hanging plastic streamers from the barbed wire on the top of his depot fence and shook his head.

'Sorry,' he said, 'but all our vehicles that aren't interstate are already booked for the parade.'

'I'd wash your trucks every Saturday morning,' said Pearl.

'Sorry,' said the manager, grinning.

Pearl resisted the temptation to stop holding his stepladder steady.

'Please,' she said, 'can't you take my name in case there's a cancellation?'

'I could,' said the manager, 'if you've got a thousand dollars deposit and a class six licence.'

Pearl sighed.

The taxi driver tucked his newspaper behind his sun visor and scratched his head.

'Run that past me again,' he said. 'What is it you want moved? Perhaps I can fit it in the boot.'

Pearl stuck her head inside the taxi so he could hear her better.

'A throne,' said Pearl. 'It's a lounge chair

really, with a big heavy curtain on it. And a senior citizen.'

The taxi driver looked at Pearl.

'We'd strap her down,' said Pearl. 'And use towels so the roof doesn't get scratched.'

The taxi driver stared at Pearl, then shook his head.

'Can't put things on the roof,' he said. 'Against regulations.'

'OK,' said Pearl, 'are you allowed to tow things? For special customers.'

The taxi driver frowned.

'I can tow,' he said, 'but only in emergencies.'

Pearl took a deep breath, leaned further into the taxi, and told him about Gran.

Chapter Thirteen

'You look beautiful, Gran,' said Pearl.
'Yeah,' said Mitch. 'You're easily the best-looking Carnival Queen.'

Gran grinned.

'Best-looking one in the Co-op carpark, anyway,' she said.

She twirled around so that Mum's living room curtains billowed out around her shoulders.

'Gold and orange aren't colours I wear a lot,' she panted, 'but what the heck, it's a special occasion.'

Pearl checked her watch.

'The parade should be leaving the sports oval now,' she said. 'They'll be here in five minutes.'

She felt Mitch nudging her.

Oops, she thought, almost forgot.

She reached into her schoolbag and lifted out the Viking helmet.

She checked that the toilet-roll horns were still stuck to the brass plant pot.

They were.

'There you go, Gran,' she said.

Gran put it on, eyes shining.

It's working, thought Pearl happily. She's looking stronger and healthier already.

If only Mum could be here to see this.

Then perhaps she'd understand why we're having to borrow her car.

Gran gripped Mitch's shoulder, climbed up onto the driver's seat of the Capri, planted her bottom on the head rest and practised waving.

No time to worry about Mum now, thought Pearl. The parade'll be here in four minutes.

She went round to the front of the car to see how the taxi driver was going with the towrope.

It was in place.

'Will it be strong enough?' asked Pearl anxiously.

'I could tow a bus with this,' said the taxi driver. 'Little open sports car'll be a snack, even with a large grandmother in it.'

Gran glared at him.

The taxi driver grinned at her and gave her a thumbs up.

Gran took a deep wheezy breath.

Stay calm Gran, begged Pearl silently. Don't

put a strain on your respiratory system.

The taxi driver checked the towrope connections.

'She's a remarkable woman,' he whispered to Pearl. 'Wish I could have done this for my Gran. So, when's your mum getting here?'

Pearl took a deep breath.

This was the moment she'd been dreading.

The moment when the whole plan could end up in the ashtray.

'She won't be,' said Pearl. 'She's got VIP guests to look after. It'll just be us.'

The taxi driver looked doubtful.

'Who's going to steer the Capri?' he said. 'You kids can't.'

For a sec Pearl thought Gran was going to have a coughing fit, but she was just clearing her throat.

'I've had my driving licence for forty-nine years,' she said.

The taxi driver still looked doubtful.

'Can you steer from up there?' he said.

Gran reached out and gripped the wheel.

'One hand for steering,' she said, 'one for waving. Now, could you get in the cab and start the meter please?'

The taxi driver didn't move.

'I hope you've got an ignition key,' he said, 'for that steering lock.'

113

Mitch gave Pearl a panicked look.

Pearl pulled Mum's spare key from her jeans pocket and handed it to the taxi driver.

Mitch still looked panicked.

Pearl realised why.

In the distance she could hear the rumble of trucks.

The parade was coming.

Pearl didn't get panicked.

Just a bit worried.

'What I'm worried about,' she said in her head to Winston, 'is that when the parade trucks see a taxi pull out in front of them towing a red sports car with two kids and a Viking gran in it, they might slam on their brakes and crash into each other and cause the parade to be cancelled and me and Mitch and Gran and the taxi driver to be arrested for obstructing traffic.'

In her head Pearl was relieved to see that Winston wasn't scampering around looking for somewhere to hide.

He was giving her his calm 'everything's going to be OK' look.

And it was.

At first.

As the taxi and the Capri pulled out in front of the parade, Pearl looked anxiously at the front truck.

114

The Carnival Queen was staring and pointing at them with her tobacco wand.

Ron and Les Piggott were waving their arms and shouting.

In Australian, not Nubian.

But the truck, and the rest of the parade behind it, kept on coming.

Pearl grinned up at Gran.

'Comfy?' she yelled.

Gran gave her a thumbs up.

Pearl had the thought that perhaps they should have strapped her in somehow. She tried to remember if the Vikings had used seatbelts.

But it was too late, the taxi was towing them round the corner into the main street.

Pearl gasped.

The crowd was huge.

At least ten deep on both sides of the street.

This is incredible, thought Pearl. Everyone in town must be here.

The cheer that went up was the loudest Pearl had ever heard, but when Gran started waving it got even louder.

People were laughing and shouting and pointing and clapping, and nobody seemed to have noticed there were two carnival queens.

Or if they had, they didn't care.

Pearl hoped the organisers were feeling the same way.

She checked to see if Gran needed a chocolate crackle to keep her energy up, but Gran seemed fine.

With her weatherbeaten face glowing with pleasure and the sun gleaming off her helmet, she looked like the carved figurehead on a Viking warship.

Indestructible, except at funerals.

Pearl hoped Gran's lungs were feeling the same way.

Halfway down the main street, Mitch tapped Pearl on the shoulder and leant forward and put his lips to her ear.

'I was wrong,' he shouted. 'This is exactly what Gran needs to keep her going till Doug gets here.'

Pearl grinned and nodded, but she didn't reply, partly because of the noise and partly because of what she'd just seen on the VIP viewing platform outside the supermarket.

Mum, very agitated, pointing at the Capri and talking loudly to a policeman.

She seemed to be urging the policeman to do something.

The policeman seemed to be saying no.

Pearl thought of Winston's lucky nose and made a wish.

That the policeman had come to the parade straight from shooting practice so his ears were still ringing so he couldn't hear people telling him to arrest their daughters.

Then Mitch gripped Pearl's shoulder and pointed to a man in a safari suit and a woman in shorts standing near Mum.

The man's mouth was open and the woman was clutching her stomach and they were both staring at Gran in horror.

'My parents have arrived,' shouted Mitch unhappily.

Pearl looked up at Gran.

She must have seen what was happening on the VIP platform too because suddenly she wasn't looking so indestructible.

Her shoulders were drooping and she was wheezing a lot.

Pearl gave her a chocolate crackle.

During the coughing fit that followed, Pearl wondered if that had been such a good idea.

Several people in the crowd reeled back with bits of chocolate crackle on their clothes.

But then Gran stopped coughing, and for the rest of her triumphant journey down the main street she had the broad shoulders and even broader grin, Pearl was delighted to see, of a woman whose lungs were probably getting better by the minute.

As they turned out of the main street, the cheers fading behind them, Gran slipped down into the driver's seat and turned to Pearl and Mitch with shining eyes.

'Thank you,' she wheezed, and pressed her wet face to theirs.

Pearl glowed.

It's worked, she thought. Nobody could be this happy and terminally ill.

After a long time, Gran stopped hugging them.

Mitch blinked and looked around.

'Where are we going?' he asked.

'To the showground,' said Pearl. 'It's where the parade ends.'

Mitch peered nervously ahead.

'Wouldn't we be better off going somewhere else?' he said. 'Where we're not, you know, expected.'

Pearl shook her head.

'We've got to face them sooner or later,' she said.

Mum and Howard and Mitch's parents were waiting at the showground.

As the Capri rolled through the gates, Pearl saw Mum's face and Pearl's guts started to roll too.

She'd never seen Mum so angry.

Mum dragged her out of the car even before it had completely stopped.

'How dare you?' shouted Mum. 'How dare you ruin my parade?'

'Do you know the penalties for car theft?' shouted Howard.

'How dare you make me a laughing stock in front of my clients?' shouted Mum.

'Jail, that's the penalty,' shouted Howard.

'Not just local clients, overseas clients,' shouted Mum.

'How do you think your mother would feel with you in jail?' shouted Howard.

'You selfish, selfish, selfish girl,' shouted Mum.

Pearl was dimly aware that Mitch was copping it from his parents.

Even though she was being shaken and deafened and sprayed with saliva, Pearl managed to glance over to see how he was.

Which is how she came to see Gran slumped motionless in the car, arm hanging over the door, face on the steering wheel.

Nobody shouted in the hospital waiting room.

Mum and Howard and Mitch's parents stared at the carpet, white-faced and silent.

Pearl wouldn't have cared if they had yelled.

All she cared about was Gran.

If I've made her worse, she thought, I'll never forgive myself.

She wondered if jails accepted people who

119

asked to be locked up for long sentences.

If they don't, she thought miserably, I'll do solitary confinement in my room for twenty years.

She could see that Mitch, sitting hunched between his parents, was feeling the same way.

When the doctor came in, Pearl was first on her feet.

'You can see her now,' said the doctor, 'but I have to warn you, she's very, very ill.'

Everyone followed the doctor.

'You stay here,' Mum snapped at Pearl.

No way, said Pearl to herself.

She followed them down the corridor at a distance.

When she got to Gran's room and peeked in, they were all standing round the bed looking at Gran, who was lying ashen-faced on a pile of pillows with several tubes connected to her.

'How are you feeling, Mum?' said Howard.

'Tops,' wheezed Gran. 'All except my body. It's a bit crook. In fact I reckon it's a goner.'

Mitch's mum took Gran's hand.

'Don't say that, Mum,' she said. 'Tomorrow morning you'll be in the air ambulance and by lunchtime you'll be in the hands of the best specialists in Australia.'

Gran took several deep wheezy breaths.

'You've all been wonderful,' she said, 'but

there's something I want to say to you all, and that specially includes Mitch and Pearl.'

Pearl realised Gran was beckoning to her.

She took a deep breath and walked into the room, trying not to meet any of the adults' eyes.

Gran beckoned her closer and took her and Mitch's hands.

'Thanks to my two wonderful grandchildren,' said Gran, 'today has been one of the best days of my life.'

Gran gave them both a painful grin.

Pearl was aware that the adults behind her were shuffling and muttering.

'And I reckon,' wheezed Gran, 'that's the best way to call it quits.'

'Nonsense Mum,' said Howard. 'You're going to be fine.'

'No, I'm not,' said Gran. 'So here's what I'm gunna do. You people in this room are all the people I love in the world. After I've said goodbye, and told you what sort of funeral I want, I'm gunna speak to the very nice people at this hospital and ask them to give me an injection somewhere where it doesn't hurt.'

The room was silent.

Pearl saw the adults glancing at each other, puzzled.

Then she realised Gran was looking straight at her.

'And after it's put me out of my misery, young lady,' said Gran with a tiny painful smile, 'I do not want to be kept in a freezer.'

Chapter Fourteen

Later, after everyone had calmed down a bit and Mum had gone to the hospital canteen with Howard to get him a cup of tea for his migraine and Mitch's dad had gone to the pharmacy with Mitch's mum to get her some antacid for her stomach, Pearl crept back into Gran's room.

Gran was asleep.

Pearl sat by the bed.

Poor thing, she thought.

No wonder you're exhausted after all that mayhem.

People weeping at you.

Pleading with you.

Waving private hospital brochures in your face.

Shouting at each other to talk sense to you.

Not listening to you.

Gran stirred and took a couple of sharp breaths and something rattled in her chest.

Pearl hoped it wasn't confetti from the parade lodged in her windpipe.

'Have a cough, Gran,' she whispered. 'Get it out.'

Gran slept on.

Pearl looked at the clear liquid in the plastic tube running into the back of Gran's hand.

She hoped it was the strongest pain killer in the whole world.

That's the least those doctors can do, thought Pearl, after treating you like that.

Lecturing you.

Quoting hospital rules at you.

Patting your hand and telling you to think of your loving family and not be a selfish girl.

And not answering, thought Pearl sadly, as she watched the tiny muscles under Gran's eyes twitch with pain, one simple question.

'Can she be cured?' asked Pearl.

The two doctors dozing in front of the TV jumped several centimetres in their vinyl arm-chairs and spilled coffee on their trousers.

They blinked and looked around and saw Pearl.

And frowned.

'This rest area is for medical staff only,' said

one. 'Visitors have to go to the canteen.'

'But they don't have to eat the food,' said the other. 'Fortunately.'

They both chuckled.

Great, thought Pearl. Gran's life is in the hands of Kermit and Fozzy.

'I just want to know if she can be cured,' said Pearl. 'Please.'

'Who are we talking about?' said the first doctor.

'My Gran,' said Pearl. 'In Room 14.'

The doctors exchanged a glance.

'She's comfortable and sleeping peacefully,' said the first doctor.

'Can she be cured?' asked Pearl.

'The hospital she's going to tomorrow,' said the first doctor, 'has the best facilities in the country.'

'Can she be cured?' asked Pearl.

The doctors looked at each other.

'It's OK,' said Pearl. 'I can take it. I've already had one close family member die recently.'

The second doctor looked at Pearl.

'No,' he said, 'she can't be cured.'

I can take it, Pearl told herself.

I can take it.

But her hands couldn't.

They started shaking.

Then the rest of her couldn't either.

After she'd stopped shaking and convinced the doctors she was OK, Pearl crept back into Gran's room.

Mitch was sitting on the bed talking to Gran.

'I'm sending him messages every five minutes,' Mitch was saying. 'Doug's a busy bloke, but he's got to check in with his secretary sooner or later. Angels have to, it's in their contract.'

Gran smiled wearily.

'Mitch,' she said, 'there's something I have to tell you about Doug.'

'No,' said Mitch, jumping off the bed. 'Don't try and tell me that bull about Doug not being real.'

He turned angrily and saw Pearl.

'She's her own worst enemy,' he said. 'How's Doug meant to save her when she won't even believe in him?'

Pearl didn't know what to say.

'I believe in him,' said Gran, 'cause I know he's real.'

Mitch stared at Gran.

Gran patted the bed.

'Both of you,' she said.

They went over to the bed and sat and waited for Gran to struggle with a rattly breath.

'When I was a kid,' said Gran, 'my parents didn't like me. Dunno why.'

She took another rusty exhaust-pipe breath.

'I turned into a bit of a ratbag. Cause of that other people didn't like me much either. Then, when I was fifteen, I met a young bloke who did. Other people reckoned he was an idiot for wasting his time with me, but he told them to boil their heads. He cared about me. Dunno why, but he did. I'll give you an example. He reckoned I could be Carnival Queen. I knew I couldn't cause I was too tall and I had a face like a boot, but he reckoned I could. Then he drowned.'

Gran struggled with another breath.

'His name,' she said to Mitch, 'was Doug.'

Pearl watched as Mitch struggled with a breath himself.

'Later on, when you were a scared little kid, Mitch,' continued Gran, 'and I wanted to tell you about someone extra special who'd be keeping an eye out for you ... well ... I prob-ably shouldn't have done, but I picked Doug.'

Gran struggled to put her hand on Mitch's arm.

With Pearl's help she managed it.

'The truth is Mitch,' said Gran, 'I don't know if Doug's an angel or not.'

Pearl held her breath while Mitch and Gran looked at each other.

'I'm sorry,' said Gran.

Mitch stood up.

'You might think Doug's just some dead bloke,' he said, eyes blazing with anger and hurt, 'but he's gunna save your life, you wait and see.'

He ran out of the room.

Gran gave a long rattly sigh.

'Poor kid,' she said, wiping her eyes. 'I'm a prize dope. I should have told him ages ago, not leave it till the end. My trouble is I don't like painful stuff. I'm an old coward.'

Pearl picked up one of Gran's big wrinkled hands.

'No you're not,' she said softly.

She held Gran's hand while Gran's breathing became slower and quieter.

When Gran had drifted into sleep, Pearl let tears fill her eyes and run down her cheeks.

She sat in the dark room like that for a long time, stroking Gran's hair until the adults came back.

Chapter Fifteen

'Stop that talk right now,' said Mum, the carton of takeaway in her hand trembling with anger, 'or I'll wash your mouth out with detergent.'

Pearl couldn't stop.

Even though she could see it was upsetting Howard, she couldn't stop for Gran's sake.

'If she wants to die,' said Pearl, 'she should be allowed to.'

Mum thumped the takeaway carton down onto the table. Beef chow mein splashed onto the wall.

'In case you've forgotten,' said Mum, 'she's Howard's mother. And I care a lot about her too and so should you.'

'That's why we have to help her,' said Pearl.

Howard reached across the table and poured himself another whisky.

'Don't talk about things you don't understand,' he said.

'We helped Winston,' said Pearl.

Howard coughed whisky into his fried rice.

'I'm warning you Pearl,' said Mum.

'Winston,' said Howard, 'was a guinea pig.'

Pearl wiped a piece of fried pork off her eyelid.

'You said it was a shame,' she said, 'to make him suffer a couple of weeks of pointless pain and misery, remember?'

'Howard's mother,' said Mum, 'is a person.'

'I know,' said Pearl.

She felt her voice wobble.

Don't start crying, she said to herself.

Gran needs you too much.

'Why can guinea pigs be saved from pointless pain and misery,' said Pearl, 'and not people?'

Howard banged his glass down onto the table. Whisky and soda splashed over the lemon chicken.

'Because doctors don't do that sort of thing,' he said. 'They can't. They're not allowed to.'

Pearl took a deep breath and looked at Howard.

'Then why don't you help her?'

'Because,' said Howard, his face dark with anguish, 'I'm a vet.'

'Pearl,' said Mum, 'go to your room.'

130

*

Pearl went to her room.

She stayed there until she heard Howard leave and Mum go to bed.

After that she stayed there another three hours, just to be on the safe side.

Then she crept into the kitchen and opened the fridge.

Sorry about the lumps, Gran, she thought as she stirred yoghurt and bran together in a glass, but I daren't use the blender.

And sorry there's no kelp or pollen.

She had the fleeting thought of ducking out the back and seeing if any of the herbs in the tub were flowering, but she decided not to.

If she was going to help Gran, it wasn't pollen she needed.

Howard's back door was unlocked.

Pearl tried to keep her sigh of relief as quiet as possible as she slipped inside.

Carefully she put the glass of health sludge on the table and shone her torch around the dark kitchen.

Please, she said to herself, please let it be in here and not under Howard's bed.

As her beam moved slowly round the room, dark shapes and wobbly shadows appeared and disappeared.

Pearl recognised the toaster and the microwave and the milk bottle carrier, but nothing that looked even remotely like a vet's bag.

She shone the torch over the whole room again.

It wasn't there.

That meant she'd have to go through the house looking for it.

A dark house she hardly knew.

With three adults asleep in it.

Pearl felt panic start to scrabble deep inside her.

It wasn't in her chest yet, but it was on its way.

She took a deep breath.

Winston, she thought.

What would you have done, Winston?

In her head Winston was looking at her with a familiar expression.

The expression he used when he was encouraging her not to be such a dope.

Then it hit her.

Of course.

The fridge.

Vets always keep some of their drugs in the fridge so they don't go off.

Pearl tore the fridge door open and there, tinkling in the butter cooler, were small glass bottles.

Holding the torch close, she studied the labels. She didn't know what half the words meant.

If only, she thought desperately, animal drug manufacturers had to put the same warning notices on their labels as cigarette manufacturers did.

THIS PRODUCT KILLS GRANDMOTHERS

Something like that.

Then Pearl saw what she was looking for.

A label that said Horse Tranquilliser.

That should do it, thought Pearl.

Gran's big, but she's nowhere near as big as a horse.

Pearl snapped the plastic top off the bottle and tipped the liquid into the glass of health sludge.

Then she went looking for a spoon to give it a stir.

She was surprised how quietly she managed to slide the cutlery drawer open.

It was so quiet she was able to hear quite clearly someone opening the kitchen door and coming in behind her.

Pearl froze.

Then she swung round with the torch.

Standing there, blinking in the circle of light, was Mitch.

They looked at each other.

Pearl felt the panic fill her chest and rush up her throat.

She waited for Mitch to yell out for someone.

His parents.

Howard.

Doug.

But he didn't.

'I've been thinking,' he said, straightening his pyjama top.

'Yes?' croaked Pearl.

'I reckon if Doug was gunna save Gran, he'd have done it by now.'

Mitch took a deep stuttering breath.

Pearl saw he'd been crying.

'I reckon,' he said, 'poor old Gran's on her own.'

'No she's not,' said Pearl. 'She's got us.'

Chapter Sixteen

The hospital was almost deserted, but Pearl didn't want to take any chances.

Not when it was a matter of life and death.

She and Mitch stood in the bushes, thinking.

'Gran's window,' whispered Mitch. 'She never sleeps with her window closed.'

'Good on you,' whispered Pearl.

She made a silent wish that whoever in the town council had decided to build a single-storey hospital should be rewarded in their life by getting heaps of love from a gran and a guinea pig.

They found Gran's room by counting the windows.

Gran's window creaked a bit when Pearl pulled it open wider.

Pearl put her hand on Mitch's arm to stop him

climbing in until she'd checked it was Gran in the bed.

It was.

Gran's eyes were closed and her mouth was open and in the pale glow of the nightlight her face looked smaller than Pearl remembered.

As Pearl swung her leg over the windowsill, a thought stabbed into her and she almost dropped the glass of health sludge.

Perhaps Gran had died already.

Pearl tried to hope she had, for Gran's sake, but she couldn't do it.

Mitch clambered in and knocked a vase over.

Gran opened her eyes.

She looked at them for a while, wheezing softly, before she spoke.

'G'day,' she said.

Then she grinned.

'I was hoping you'd come.'

Pearl held out the sludge.

'We've brought you something,' she said.

'Yeah,' said Mitch.

Gran tried to chuckle, but it turned into a cough.

Pearl saw Gran's face crease with pain.

'Thanks,' said Gran, 'you're both champs, but I'm a bit past that now.'

'It's instead of the injection,' said Pearl.

Gran looked at them for a long time.

'You're not just champs,' she said at last, 'you're angels. But I'm pretty much past that too. No point getting you into trouble when nature's doing the job for us.'

Gran coughed again and Pearl watched helplessly as Gran's face twisted in agony.

She held the glass closer to Gran.

'Drink it, please,' she said.

'We want to help you,' said Mitch.

Gran looked at them, panting painfully.

'I don't need you to help me cark it,' she said, 'but I could use a hand with the travel arrangements.'

When they got to the lake, dawn was just starting to break.

'All the best,' said the taxi driver softly.

Pearl realised he was speaking to all of them.

He touched Gran on the arm for a moment, then reached for the note Gran had written.

'If anyone comes,' he said, 'I'll have this ready.'

Pearl and Mitch helped Gran down to the water's edge.

'On my back,' wheezed Gran.

They lowered her into the water.

As Gran started to float, the hospital nightie billowing out around her, Pearl saw Gran's whole body relax.

'If you can manage it,' said Gran, 'I'd like to go to the middle.'

'I can manage it,' said Pearl.

'What about you, Mitch?' said Gran.

'I'll try,' said Mitch.

Pearl launched herself into the water, kicking gently, steering Gran out towards the centre of the lake.

She saw that Mitch was hanging on to the other side of Gran, face tense with concentration, kicking furiously.

'Not too hard Mitch,' croaked Gran, 'or we'll go round in circles.'

'Sorry,' panted Mitch.

They moved slowly through the silver water.

Pearl realised Gran wasn't wheezing any more, and when she spoke her voice was clear and soft.

'I'm not gunna say goodbye,' said Gran, 'cause you know where I'll be.'

Pearl nodded.

She glanced across at Mitch.

He was nodding too.

Gran didn't speak again, and when they finally arrived at the centre of the lake, the water fiery with the first rays, Pearl saw that Gran had stopped breathing.

Her face was calm and expectant, as if she was about to see someone she loved very much.

'Mitch,' said Pearl softly, 'it's time to let go.'

They let go.

Slowly, arms spreading in welcome, Gran slipped from sight.

Then Pearl remembered Mitch couldn't swim.

She looked anxiously over at him.

He wasn't thrashing around in distress.

He was on his back, gazing at the sky with an amazed, tear-streaked face.

Floating.

Pearl rolled over and floated next to him.

She closed her eyes and out of the warm darkness of her tears, two familiar faces appeared, smiling at her.

'Winston,' she said, 'I'd like you to meet Gran.'

In the distance Pearl could hear the sound of vehicles, and people shouting.

She took Mitch's hand and they headed for the shore.

Morris Gleitzman titles
available from Macmillan

The prices shown below are correct at the time of going to press.
However, Macmillan Publishers reserve the right to show new retail
prices on covers which may differ from those previously advertised.

MORRIS GLEITZMAN

Misery Guts	0 330 32440 3	£3.99
Worry Warts	0 330 32845 X	£3.99
Puppy Fat	0 330 34211 8	£3.99
Blabber Mouth	0 330 39777 X	£4.99
Sticky Beak	0 330 39778 8	£4.99
Belly Flop	0 330 39824 5	£4.99
Water Wings	0 330 39825 3	£4.99

All Macmillan titles can be ordered at your local bookshop
or are available by post from:

Book Service by Post
PO Box 29, Douglas, Isle of Man IM99 1BQ

Credit cards accepted. For details:
Telephone: 01624 675137
Fax: 01624 670923
E-mail: bookshop@enterprise.net

Free postage and packing in the UK.
Overseas customers: add £1 per book (paperback)
and £3 per book (hardback).